Crushed Velvet and Cashmere

K.L. HALL

#BLP

Synopsis

"They call me Kas," he whispered in my ear.

I clenched my thighs. He smelled of warm vanilla and musk with a hint of marijuana.

From his enigmatic eyes to the neck tattoo that extended past the crisp fold of his collared shirt, he screamed danger.

And without the resolve to fight against the pressure to mix business with pleasure, I slipped right underneath his thumb and into his dark world.

All I *wanted* to do was scale my interior design business to the next level.
All I *needed* was a client who was paid.

I didn't want to fall so violently for him.
I didn't need the keys to his heart.

Now I may just lose my sanity because of it.

"You got me open when everything closed."
-Wale

One

JRUE NORWOOD

MY HIPS instinctively swayed to the bass from the club speakers rattling the cheap vanity mirror in the dressing room. After closing the clasps on my oversized hoop earrings, I swiped my hands down my work "uniform," a strappy black dress that fit me tighter than a fresh pack of Newports. I leaned closer to the mirror to readjust the bobby pin in my top knot bun, while the rest of my honey blonde and black passion twists swayed against the tip of my ass.

"Jrue, Whip is looking for you. He said if you don't get your ass over to your VIP section, tonight will be the night he fires your black ass," one of the other bottle girls warned me.

I smacked my lips, knowing damn well I wanted to tell Whip he could keep this sorry-ass job, but he and I both knew that I needed the pay. "Aight. Tell him I'm coming out in a minute. I just gotta reapply my lipstick."

"Yeah, aight."

I quickly brushed my finger underneath my long, coal lashes, giving them a quick fluff, before reapplying my cognac brown lipstick. I gave myself one last once over before tossing my lipstick back into my makeup bag and shoving it inside my locker. *Aight, Jrue girl. Let's go get this money*, I thought to myself.

The moment my heels clicked and clacked out onto the scene, the potent aroma of money, ass, and marijuana fanned past my nose. My eyes scanned the entire first floor as I braced myself for another night catering to Philly's elite street clientele via bottle service in the VIP areas. Trap music blasted out of the speakers as girls from wall to wall twisted around on the poles as if they were auditioning for Cirque du Soleil. Others were shaking their titties and vibrating their asses so hard on the floor that it was enough to start an earthquake. Bliss was like the X-rated Disney World for all of Philly's ballers.

As cliché as the name may have been, Bliss wasn't the seedy ass hole in the wall pretending like it sounded better than what it could be. From the lavishly themed rooms to the 1,500-bottle wine cellar, it screamed class, luxury, and *big* money. It wasn't for the broke or faint at heart, and that was precisely why I worked here. Being a bottle girl alongside all my other odd-end jobs was just a steppingstone until I could scale my interior decorating business, Jrue's Interiors, to the next level. I was an entrepreneur at heart. My business was my baby, and launching it was a dream come true, but I'd be lying if I said being a young Black female entrepreneur was easy. I was tired of taking on clients with Prada ideas and Big Lots budgets. My most challenging feat had been finding ways to gain the visibility of potential clients who had the means to align with their big ideas. Taking the job at Bliss was my way of trying to find high-paying clientele so I could start to build a visually diverse portfolio.

I waltzed over to the bar where Whip stood with a smug look across his aging brown face. "What took you so long?"

"You can't rush perfection," I reminded him.

He rolled his beady brown eyes. "Yeah, whatever. The section upstairs just filled up with a new party. I know I don't have to tell you this, but—"

"Yeah, yeah, I know. *Don't fuck it up.* Don't worry. I won't."

Whip may have been an asshole to work for, but he knew his business. He took everything he hated from all the other clubs around the city and even the tri-state area and made sure the one he owned was ten times better. The drinks? Strong enough to put hair on your chest. The girls? Exotic and stacked on legs like stallions. The décor? Modern and sleek. The parking? Valet for VIP or a flat thirty-dollar fee plus the price of admission. The food? Five-star, finger lickin' good. Whip wanted all of Philly's hustlers and the surrounding areas to feel like royalty as soon as they stepped inside so they'd effortlessly hand over every single one of their hard-earned dollars.

"Who's working the section with me tonight?" I asked him.

"Nobody, it's just you."

My brows crushed together in disapproval. "Just me?" I asked, pointing to myself.

"Yeah. Kara called out sick again. I think the bitch got the flu or somethin'. Now hop to it. You know my patrons don't want to be kept waiting for shit."

I rolled my eyes, knowing I would be in for one hell of a long night that ended with aching feet and an Epsom salt soak at four o'clock in the morning. With my tray in hand, I made my way up to my section, griping all the way. The moment I got up there, I was met with the smell of tequila as hundreds of one-dollar bills floated in the air. My eyes were met with a section full of gangsters with twenty-two different shades of brown asses shaking all in their faces. I drew in a sharp breath and then exhaled slowly. *Why the fuck didn't I hit my weed pen before I left the locker room?* I thought to myself.

I surveyed the section and saw a man looking like he would've rather been anywhere in the world than in the sea of ass and titties that were currently swimming around him. The strobe lights flashed against his mahogany brown skin, illuminating it in the darkness as I edged closer. Knowing I needed to talk to someone about what bottles they wanted for their section, I figured he may have been the least drunk and abrasive one to talk to. From the looks of it, he seemed to be well-groomed. I couldn't see much outside of the single mole on his right cheek, the jet-black mustache, and the full beard covering the entire lower half of his face that looked as soft as cotton.

"Hey, you look like you need a pick me up. Can I get you anything? Patrón? Henny?" I asked him.

He shook his head before pulling his umber brown eyes up to meet mine. "Nah, I'm good. Two drinks in my system are my limit."

"A limit? I thought you were celebrating."

"I thought you were supposed to encourage me to drink responsibly," he said, flashing a preview of his perfectly aligned white teeth.

"Not if it means you'll tip better if you're wasted," I joked.

He let out a muted chuckle before licking his smooth, pouty lips. "Funny."

"I was supposed to come over and ask what bottles you wanted for your section, but unlike your friends over there, you look like you need a cup of coffee instead of more liquor," I said, referring to the niggas standing on the couches next to him with bottles of liquor permanently attached to their hands.

He turned his attention to them, allowing me to catch a glimpse of the neck tattoo etched into his flesh and the oversized diamond settled inside his small earlobe. Both sides of his head and the back were shaven low, while his hair on top was long enough to braid down or wear in a man bun. He currently had it braided down in small, neat braids.

"Let 'em have their fun, and bring 'em whatever they want."

"And what about you? What do you want?" I asked him.

"To know your name," he said.

My mocha brown eyes popped wide for a split second before I responded. "Jrue. My name is Jrue. What's yours?" I yelled over the music.

He leaned his body into mine. "They call me Kas." He whispered in my ear.

I clenched my thighs. He smelled of warm vanilla and musk with a hint of marijuana. From his enigmatic eyes to the neck tattoo that extended past the crisp fold of his collared shirt, he screamed danger. I immediately felt the hairs rise on the back of my neck as every set of female eyes in the section landed dead on us. They began twerking harder, vying for his attention while giving me daggered green-eyed stares.

I took a few safety steps away from him, putting six feet between us. "I'll go ahead and get those bottles. You need to start throwing dollars before shit starts getting real in here."

"Why I gotta throw dollars just because we're at a strip club?"

"Don't you know you and your wallet are in shark-infested waters right now? So, when in Rome..."

He flashed a full smile that time, weakening me instantly. "Guess I'll do what the Romans do," he replied.

"Good. I'll be back shortly."

Two

KASIM "KAS" BARNES

JRUE'S SCENT of brown sugar and shea lingered long after she'd left my presence. I was so intrigued that I allowed my eyes to follow her as she made her way down to the bar. I leaned over the balcony and studied her as she prepared the bottles for our section and parted through the mass of patrons and poles alike, with flickering sparks attached to large liquor bottles to light her path. Usually, I wouldn't have been caught out politicking with every nigga in the city who pushed a Benz or had a stack in their pocket, but it was my older brother's bachelor party, and I was determined to show him a good time. Meeting Jrue only seemed to be the icing on the cake for me. Even through those sexy, coy ass smiles she kept giving me, I could tell she was far from innocent. She was a natural beauty with walnut bronzed skin, a cupid's bow on her top lip, and devilishly inviting eyes. All I could think about was how good those long-ass twists she was rockin' would look wrapped around my fingers.

Before I could approach her again, my younger brother, Kamil, slammed his drunk ass body into mine, hooking his arm around my shoulder. "You havin' fun, nigga?" he asked, the smell of tequila and lime hopping off his tongue.

"Don't worry about me. What about you? Are you havin' a good time? You and Koda ain't had a free lap or hand since we got in this mothafucka," I told him.

Koda joined us, barging in on our conversation. Both of them were drunk as skunks. "You mothafuckin right I'm havin' a good fuckin' time! It's my last night as a free man, and I'm going to enjoy the fuck outta myself and get my dick as wet as I want tonight!" He boasted before pulling his long, jet-black dreads back into a ponytail.

I shook my head. Although we were two years apart, I was the middle child and closest to Kamil, who was three years younger than me. Mentally, I was light years ahead of them both. As reckless and disorderly as he was acting, I understood it.

He was set to marry Cena McQueen, daughter of Silas McQueen, a big name in Philly's drug scene. According to our father, their marriage would strengthen the bond between our families. While Koda was marrying for family, Kamil had been lucky enough to marry for love. He'd been in love with Janessa Underwood since they were teenagers. So, it was nothing for him to put a ring on it, especially when she was from a family that worked alongside ours. I was happy he'd found someone who understood our lifestyle and all that came with it without the need to ask a lot of questions. His wedding was set to follow soon after Koda's. I couldn't believe he was excited about tying himself down to one woman for the rest of his life, but as long as he was happy about it, then so was I.

"Do whatever you want tonight; just be safe. I ain't tryna have to kill nobody over you two tonight, nigga," I warned.

"Loosen up, Kas. Shit, everything is all love tonight. Have some fun. Get you a drink and some pussy or somethin', aight?" Koda advised.

I chuckled. "Yo, those two drinks are runnin' through a nigga. I'ma head to the bathroom, and then we need to be out in another thirty minutes max. A nigga still gotta get you down that aisle in one piece like I promised."

Koda frowned. "Nigga, don't kill my vibe."

I patted him on his back and went to the bathroom. On my way back to my section, I saw Jrue heading toward the bar. I changed course and met her in the middle of the dance floor.

I called out to her over the music. "Yo."

"Look who managed to stay awake after all?" She chuckled.

"Yeah, and somehow you're still floatin' around in those four-inch heels with grace."

"Trust me; it takes a certain amount of mastered patience to deal with drunk ass niggas every night. I'm not floating gracefully; you're just seeing double or something. Besides, most niggas don't care what I look like buzzing back and forth through here. They're all determined to play out the fantasy of bringing home the sexy stripper, bottle girl, or bartender like the T-Pain song. But let me stop rambling on and on. Can I get you anything?" she asked as we approached my section.

"I don't need shit but your company tonight, Jrue."

Her long lashes fluttered upwards, revealing the mystery in her eyes. "Well, you're lucky because I happen to be great at keeping people company."

Jrue followed me back to my section, and we talked shit for the next forty-five minutes. In a short amount of time, I learned her full name was Jrue Solène Norwood, she was twenty-five years old, the oldest of two, and a Philly jawn born and bred.

"I'm probably gon' fuck around and get fired from being up here all this time," she admitted.

"Why you don't sound like you give a fuck about somethin' like that happenin'?" I quizzed.

"This is not my only job, and it's damn sure not what I wanna do for the rest of my life."

"Oh yeah? What you wanna do?"

She rolled those beautiful brown eyes of hers. "A bitch got goals or whatever!" She smacked her lips before belting out a cute laugh.

"Tell me your goals then, Jrue."

"Well, I launched my interior design business, Jrue Interiors, a little over a year ago. I do great work and shit, but it's hard to attract the type of clientele I need to get me to that next level so I don't have to work jobs like this, you know?"

"Yeah, I do. You got a website?"

"Yeah, it's w-w-w-dot-jrueinteriors.com. Oh, and that's J-R-U-E. Check it out, and if you or any of your rich baller friends need somebody to redo a room, a house, a store, a business, or anything, tell them to holla at your girl."

"Your name is Jrue with a J and not a D. I've never seen that before."

"Yeah, most people think it's weird."

"I think it's sexy," I admitted.

She smiled bright and wide. "You're the one with the cool three-letter name, *Kas*."

I shrugged. "My full name is Kasim."

"That's a nice name too."

Knowing it was on me to respond and keep the conversation flowing as it had been, I parted my lips to speak. Before my thought could make its way off my tongue, I heard Kamil's voice loud and clear over the music.

"What the fuck did you just say to me, nigga?" He yelled before shoving a nigga I'd never seen before, knocking him back three steps.

I instinctively sprang to my feet and rushed over to Kamil's side. I didn't know who was stupid enough to have beef with us, but I was serious when I said I didn't want to have to body a nigga. "Is there a fuckin' problem here?"

"Fuck this nigga. He tried to invite himself into our section because there's a bitch he wants in here. I told the bitch nigga to get the fuck gone, and he wanted to get bold and brush my fuckin' shoulder when he was walkin' away. I'm about to show him who the fuck he's fuckin' with." Kamil growled.

"You done fucked up now," Koda warned, stepping ahead of Kamil.

"Let's go. It's time to go," I commanded, grabbing my brothers' shoulders. They were both snapping and growling like pits on a short leash.

Without having the chance to say goodbye to Jrue, I rounded up everyone who'd come with us and headed toward the blaring red exit sign. I pushed open the front doors. Just as the sole of my Ferragamos hit the curb, gunshots rang out around us in surround sound. From the second I heard the first gunshot, everything else seemed to unfold in slow motion. I looked the masked gunman in the eyes, and he looked right back into mine before letting bullets spray through the air like fireworks on July fourth. With my tight grip on Kamil, I propelled his bare cheek and mine to the cold pavement for safety. My body tensed. Without my gun, I was powerless.

Heels clicked, chains jingled, and horns honked, all contributing to the chaos that instantly engulfed us. I drew in a sharp breath, which could've easily been my last. Seconds later, the gunfire ceased. My chest rose and fell with rapid breaths as I heard the screeching of the tires as they spun down the road just before the last few shells hit the concrete around me. Beads of sweat moistened my forehead as my alarms sounded off throughout my body. Kamil and I slowly pulled ourselves back onto our feet before doing a 360-degree turn. Inches from Kamil lay a bullet casing and our brother Koda with two bullet holes in his chest. Kamil ran over to grab him just in time to watch the last flicker of life fade from his eyes.

"Koda! Koda? No! Wake up, bul! Wake the fuck up!" Kamil screamed into his chest.

Cars continued to rush by, trying to escape with their lives as sirens whirred in the distance. I stood frozen, unable to process my brother's lifeless body lying at my feet. It wasn't until I could see the red and blue lights reflecting off the dark pavement that I started to get the feeling back in my legs.

"We gotta get the fuck outta here, Kamil. Help me get 'em to the car!" I told him.

As badly as I wanted to say goodbye to Jrue, I didn't know if those bullets were meant for us or if niggas were just out doin' nigga shit because it was the weekend. Going back inside that club would be nothing but trouble, and I had to make sure we made it out safe, along with Koda's body. When we returned to the car, we sped to the emergency room, where he was officially pronounced dead on arrival.

The organ in my chest stopped beating for a few seconds. "Man, fuckkkkkkkk!" I roared, sweeping my hands over my tear-filled eyes.

"Heads are gonna fuckin' roll now. Believe that," Kamil foreshadowed, wiping tears from his eyes.

I tipped my chin. "Hell yeah. Call Pa and give him the news. I'll be back."

I walked down the hallway and charged back to the parking lot to my car. I opened the door to see his crimson blood stains on my seats and lost it. Niggas thought they could take my brother and that I wouldn't find them and seek revenge. I knew everyone expected the worst from me because they knew the type of man my father trained me to be. They knew I showed no mercy. My thoughts looped 'round and 'round like a rollercoaster. I couldn't believe Koda was gone. I felt shame for not protecting him, for not reacting sooner. Evil coursed through my veins, spreading through my body like a cancer that wouldn't stop growing. In the midst of my breakdown, I thought about Jrue and immediately wondered if she was okay. After one interaction with her on what turned out to be the craziest night of my life, I was hooked. Since I knew I wouldn't be returning to the club anytime soon, I pulled out my phone to look up her website, planning to check up on her another way.

Three

JRUE

Four days later

I SMOOTHED my clammy palms down my dusty blue dress pants and adjusted the matching blazer before taking one last glimpse at myself in my rearview mirror. With the swoop of my fingertip, I made sure my baby hairs were laid to a T before stepping out of my car and walking into the café across the street. The bell chimed against the door as I made my way inside the brick-and-mortar establishment. I scanned the room, searching for an open booth to grab before my potential client arrived for our consultation.

It was the first initial design consult I'd had in three months, and I was dying to take on a new project after being stood up on my last two client discovery calls. All I could hope was that whoever they were, they had the bank to match the vision. Even with tens of thousands of tiny butterflies floating around in my stomach, I still managed to keep a smile on my face and my blouse free of pit stains. I glanced down at my phone; it was 2:06 p.m. The client was supposed to meet me at two o'clock sharp. Immediately, my posture tensed, and I began feeling anxious that I was being stood up again. I quickly grabbed my laptop and went through my email to find the inquiry sent through my website. Before I could find it, my eyes shot toward the door when the bell chimed again.

"Kas?" I blurted out as he started making his way over to me.

My name fell off his lips with a half-cocked smile. "Jrue."

"W-what? I'm a little confused."

"What's there to be confused about?"

"I'm supposed to be meeting a potential client here for a consultation, but instead, you show up..."

"You're here to meet me. I'm the potential client."

"*You* need an interior decorator?" I asked, arching a suspicious brow.

"I do, and you said that if I ever needed one, to holla, right? So here I am," he said before taking his seat across from me.

I twisted my lips to delay the cockeyed smile that was dying to spread my lips from cheek to cheek. "Okay, fine. Well, since you're here, I'm glad you're okay. What happened down at the club that night was crazy."

"Yeah, it was."

"Did everybody you came with make it out okay?"

"My younger brother and I are fine, but we did lose someone."

I lowered my eyes. "I'm sorry."

"Yeah," he said with a nod. "I'm sorry we didn't get to finish our conversation or say goodbye. My family can be a little hotheaded."

"And you're not? You looked like you were really about to give it to niggas in there."

He flashed a shy grin my way, and I immediately felt the butterflies return to torment my stomach once again.

"I must admit, I did want to check on you, but I didn't know how else to find you."

"Looks like you found me just fine. So uh, why don't you tell me about this project of yours."

"Before I do that, you mentioned that night at the club that it wasn't your only job. What else do you do?"

"I think the better question is, what else don't I do? Let's see; I'm a part-time babysitter and bookshelf builder. I taught a yoga class downtown and was also a part-time dog walker until I developed an allergy to

Bedlington Terriers. They're rare, but you'd be surprised how many there are in the city."

"Damn, all those jobs, huh?"

I shrugged. "What can I say? I have a knack for making money. It's what I gotta do to get the bills paid until this interior gig starts taking off."

"Yeah, I've got a knack for money making, too, so I admire your hustle."

I blushed. "Well, thank you."

"Shit, I can't believe you actually build shit for people."

"I mean, not by hand, but as long as it has directions, I'm pretty handy with an allen wrench," I boasted.

He chuckled. "Word? I'll keep that in mind."

"So, do you want to tell me about the project now? Or I could talk more about me and my craziness."

"I could listen to you talk about your craziness all day, but what I wanna know is your design experience. How long have you been doing it?"

"Officially, a little over a year. Unofficially, I've been consulting and freelancing for the past four years. Like I told you that night, I'm ready to take my business to the next level. I'm just looking for that next big break, you know? I'm tryna make it to that next tax bracket. My overall goal for my business is to be a vibe, you know? Because I feel like, as your designer, it's my job to envision and produce vibes."

"Okay, so if we did decide to work together, walk me through your process."

I knew he wasn't going to just hand it to me. I had to sell myself, so I sat up straight and cleared my throat. "Sure. So usually, I would meet directly with you before, during, and after working on whatever the space is for your project. So, once all the paperwork and formalities are out of the way, we'd meet, and I'd gather all the information I'd need, like your budget, the timeline I'd have to get the project done, and any aesthetic preferences you might have. I'm involved in every step of the creative process, from putting the concept together from scratch to procuring the materials and staging. I do it all."

"All that sounds good."

"On top of that, I'm detail-oriented and good at multitasking because you've seen me in action. I'm good at networking because, if not, you wouldn't even be here right now. I'm focused, I'm resourceful and good at repurposing things, I have a photographic memory, and as an added bonus, I know some basic first aid."

"I bet you can do wonders with a band-aid, huh?"

"Oh, absolutely." I chuckled. "My goal isn't just to meet but to exceed your expectations."

He flaunted his contagious smile at me again. He was different from how he was at the club. Still refined but more about his business. I wanted to be professional, but I still found it easy to talk to him as if I'd known him all my life. All I could do was hope that he was taking what I was saying to be true and considering giving me a chance. Just from the tab he'd racked up at the club, I knew he would be my first big client with bank. He was just what I needed to take Jrue's Interiors to the next level.

"I think I may have something for you, but I would need to know how much time you'd have to dedicate to it with all your other jobs."

"Well, that depends on what the project is, your vision, and of course, your budget. I can drop them all if you're comfortable with my pricing. What's the job?"

"I'm months away from wrapping up my luxury condo project and need a new interior decorator. We'll start you off with a few condos on the twentieth floor, which we'll show to potential buyers. If I like your work, we'll discuss expanding to the lobby and possibly other common areas throughout the property."

My eyes lit up in delight. "I would love to work on something like that. What's your budget? When can I see the space? What's the time-frame?" I asked, practically all in one breath.

"I would need the model done quickly. It's got three bedrooms with a sky view. I'm talking about beautiful ceiling-to-floor windows equipped with the latest smart home technology, so it has to feel just as sexy as it will look. We open for showings in four months."

"I can do sexy, and I don't mind having to work quickly. That's not a problem at all," I assured him.

"Good. We'll meet to discuss your ideas on Thursday evening over dinner. If I like what you pitch, then we can move forward."

"This Thursday?" I asked. "That's in two days."

His chin descended in a nod, not seeing a damn thing wrong with what he'd just said to me. "I know it is."

"Okay, yes. I can be ready in two days. I *will* be ready in two days."

"I'll have my assistant reach out with details. It was nice seeing you again, *Miss* Norwood."

The little lightbulb in my head went off, and I laughed at his not-so-subtle way of asking me if I was married. "You can just call me Jrue, Kasim."

"Only if you call me Kas."

I nodded as my lips squirmed to the side. "Deal."

Four

KAS

JRUE'S beautiful face flickered through my mind off and on the day of Koda's funeral. From how she talked, I knew she knew her shit, which was a plus. I appreciated how thorough she was and how transparent she'd been with me. Truth be told, I'd only made her think she had to prove herself to me, but the job was hers the moment I saw her. I would've said or done anything just to keep her in my presence because I wanted to know everything about her. She was the first woman to hold my interest for more than a few days. I hadn't gone a day without thinking about her since we met, so having her where I could see her at my leisure was a win.

Leaving the burial site, I hurried to my car without saying a word to anyone. My body slid against my polar-white Mercedes' cool, honey wheat leather seats. I got rid of my old car two days after losing Koda. I had to. I could barely stand to look in my rearview anytime I drove it. All I would ever see was his lifeless body laying across it, bleeding out. Before losing him, I hadn't known grief, and didn't know the first thing about dealing with the shit, even after losing our mother at a young age. My mother divorced my father when I was five. Two days after their divorce was final, she was killed in a head-on collision. Most of the memories I had of her were stories from Koda, who was gone now too. I thought about what the two of them were doing up in heaven together. If they kicked it every day and caught up on lost time or felt more like strangers than mother and son. After putting my car in drive, Kamil's name popped up on my dashboard screen. I accepted the call and waited to hear his voice on the other line.

"Yo."

"Why you dip out so early? Pa wanted to speak with us."

"I had to get the fuck outta there and get me some air," I answered him.

"You comin' back to the house, right?"

"Yeah, I'll be there."

"Okay. I'm on my way there now with Nessa."

"What does he want to talk about?"

"I don't know what the fuck is going on, but he sounded serious."

I let out an aggravated sigh. "Aight, I'm headed over now."

I **TOOK** my time getting to my father's mansion. I meant what I said to Kamil. I needed the fresh air. My car alarm chirped as I walked past Kamil's two-seater Porsche and made my way through the maze of luxury cars up to the front door. I'd been keeping my head down and grieving the loss of my brother in silence all day. The last thing I wanted to do was be around more people who wanted to talk about how sad they were about losing Koda when they didn't really know him. I planned to hear my father out and leave.

I stepped inside, shuffling a few steps across the marble floor before seeing Kamil sitting behind the cocaine-white grand piano in the foyer. At the same time, other generals from our family's organization babbled in their side conversations. The room fell quiet when everyone noticed my father cascading down the grand staircase with the tips of his middle finger and thumb kissing to form the letter O and holding it over his heart. Every one of us returned the gesture in silence.

The Order or *"The O"* was a syndicate of six prominent crime families that joined together over ninety years ago to limit the competition on drugs, assault weapons, black market technology, and more from

Philly to states across the Northeast region, thus creating generational wealth and power. The Rivera and Massey families had territories in New York and Connecticut while the Palmer family oversaw territory in Delaware and Rhode Island, leaving parts of Jersey, Philly, and all of Pennsylvania split between the McQueen, Underwood, and Barnes families. I was the second-born son of Julius Barnes, head of the Barnes family. Now that Koda was gone, when the day came that my father's eyes closed forever, I would be the heir to one of the most powerful families in Philly's underworld.

As the son of a real OG, I was raised in the realm of danger, drugs, and black-market dealings. I lived a darker life than most. When I was eleven, I watched my father suffocate a man with plastic wrap simply because he scuffed his shoe. When I was seventeen, he handed me a gun and told me to bring him back his enemy's body. He nurtured the three of us with violence, sheltered us with privilege, and bathed us in excess. Although becoming the boss was my birthright, he ensured I'd earned every stripe over the years.

He nodded to Kamil and me, and we followed him back to his private study. The walk to the back of the house seemed to drag on until we reached the heavy wooden door. He reached for the knob, pausing for a second before proceeding inside. I drew in a deep breath, preparing for whatever news awaited us on the other side. Once the thick mahogany door closed, Kamil walked to the closest chair and took his seat while I remained on my feet.

"Take a seat, Kasim. We have important business to discuss," my father declared.

His eyes pierced mine. Looking at him was like looking into a crystal ball to see what I'd look like in thirty more years. Same height. Same ruthless mentality. He was just a lighter version of me, even down to his beard, which was still just as full as mine but salt and pepper colored.

"What's going on, Pa?" Kamil asked.

"Yeah, what's so important?" I followed up before turning my attention to the bookcase filled with books from all over the world.

"We got word about the incident that went down at the club. It was an ordered hit from Douglass Simms, head of a rival crime family. As you know, not only did we lose Koda that night, but Donovan

McQueen was also killed in the crossfire. He was transported to the hospital and died on the table in surgery. And that's—that's on me... all of this is on me," he confessed.

"How is any of this on you?" I quizzed, eyes locked on him.

His nostrils expelled a long sigh. "I fucked up."

"How?"

"I shouldn't have moved so quicky, but I thought—"

My brows knitted. "Hold up. What did you do, Pa?"

He took turns eyeing both of us in silence before parting his lips. "I've been trying to expand our reach into part of the McQueen territory for a long time. After some back and forth, Silas and I negotiated the alliance of our families through the marriage of our children. In exchange, I would move in on his territory and expand. Everything was set to move forward with their wedding, and then... Koda died."

"I'm not following any of this," I told him.

Kamil shook his head. "Yeah. Me either."

His eyes shot toward the door before his lips parted. "What no one knows is I made a lucrative business deal with the Simms family to have his men start dealing in the territory I got from Silas for a cut each month, but they moved in *before* the wedding. And since the deal with Silas wasn't finalized, McQueen's soldiers retaliated, and I—I didn't call them off."

I tilted my head to the side, eyes wide as saucers. "Are you saying the Simms family did the drive-by at the club as retaliation over a deal that *you* made?"

His eyes misted with tears as he placed his open hand over his heart. His throat grumbled before he continued. "They wanted to hit some of McQueen's men back and hit Koda in the crossfire."

The room fell silent. "I shouldn't have moved so quickly, but I told Douglass to wait for my call. I don't know why the fuck he chose to move in so fast," he grumbled.

"What made you think you could trust an enemy? Why would you even make a crazy deal like that?"

"Yeah, Pa. Why would you agree to let the enemy move in on ally territory? Are you trying to start a war?"

"Neither of you may see this now, but I'm doing what's best for business."

"Or for yourself," I mumbled.

His brow furrowed. "What the fuck did you say to me, boy?"

It was the first time I'd seen my father vulnerable and make a mistake that big. It was the first time I wasn't able to follow his mindset and understand why he made the moves he did. He'd always taught us to handle the game like chess and not checkers. But Koda's death was something he could never take back, and I didn't know if I could forgive him for the role he played in it all, even if he wasn't the one who pulled the trigger.

I cleared my throat. "Who else knows about this?" I asked, changing the subject.

"No one but the three of us in this room."

"What do you plan to do about the Simms' hit? They took Koda from us. We can't let this be forgiven," Kamil declared.

"We're not going to do anything yet," our father confirmed.

"Why not? You think they could attack again?"

I shook my head, speaking up before my father had a chance to. "They won't. They'll be waiting for us to hit back first."

"We will wait to strike until after the wedding, but if Douglass Simms chooses to retaliate first, then—"

"Then what?" Kamil questioned.

My jaw tightened before I answered. "Then I'll handle him myself."

"Wait—wait to strike after my wedding to Janessa?"

Our father bobbed his head. "Yes. I don't want to risk anything else going wrong. But speaking of marriages, that's another thing I have to talk to you two about."

"What else is there?"

Pa sighed. "Losing Koda means no one to marry Silas McQueen's daughter, Cena. And we can't afford to have another rift right now."

The room fell silent once again. My brother and I both knew that families in *The Order* believed in marriage agreements to strengthen alliances and ensure our generational wealth continued. I hadn't considered what would happen now that he was gone.

"So what do you want us to do?" Kamil asked, cutting straight to the chase.

His eyes cut from Kamil to me. "You know they want justice for what happened to Donovan just as much as we do for your brother. But now that Koda is gone, you will need to take his place, Kasim."

My heart damn near kicked a hole in my chest. "Hold up, what?"

Amid my outburst of contempt, he continued. "We agreed that you two must remain wed for six months before you can consider an annulment. They are on their way over. Silas, his daughter, Cena, and her twin brother, Canaan, to pay their respects and to discuss new wedding arrangements. I'd like to have you on board with the new plan before then."

"I'm not getting married!" I yelled. "There's gotta be somethin' else. Let me talk to Silas myself!"

My assertion fell on deaf ears. "You know what kind of family you come from, and you know our code of honor," he reminded me.

I tipped my head before raking my hand through my beard. "Blood and loyalty above all else," I stated militantly.

"What's done is done, Kas. There's no time to figure out anything else. No matter what, you will take your brother's place, and she will become your bride in six months to allow enough time for both families to grieve our losses."

I swung my head in a no until my neck grew tired. "Hell no! No! I'm not doing this! I'm not marrying her!" I protested until my mouth ran dry.

"I'm not going to repeat myself again."

"You just sat here and told us that you made a secret deal with a known rival family for money and in return, that got our brother killed! And now you want me to just take his place like it's nothing?"

He jumped across his desk, balling my collar with his fist. "I let your ass slide the first time, but you must've forgotten who the fuck you're talkin' to, boy! You better wake the fuck up from whatever dream world you're living in and get your head back in this fuckin' game. You're twenty-seven fuckin' years old, Kasim! And you oughta know by now that when I call on you, your ass is gon' answer in whatever way I tell you to or face the consequences!" he snarled, inches away from my face.

He released my crinkled shirt, shoving me backward in the process. I was sure our shouting match could be heard from the other end of the hallway, but I didn't care.

I bit the side of my cheek. "I'm sorry, Pa. But—"

"This new arrangement solidifies our loyalty, and once we come together to take down the Simms family, it will bring peace to us and the McQueens."

"Okay, but can we please just—"

"The deal has been made!" he yelled, slamming his fist onto the oak desk. "You will fuckin' marry Cena McQueen in six months. Now get the fuck out!" he barked.

My father had simply tried to slip me into my brother's place as if no one would notice, like a pawn on a board. So much for being the heir to an empire. With all the power I wielded at my fingertips, I had no choice or say-so in how my life would go. My thoughts swam laps around my head as I charged out of his study. The only way out would be to leave the city and everything I'd ever known behind, including my family and the throne. The doorbell chimed, which told me I'd run out of time. I didn't even have a second to process what the fuck had just happened before my father went to greet more guests who'd come to pay their respects. My head hung low as I silently shoved down all my unwanted feelings.

"Yo, Kas—you aight, man?" Kamil asked, pushing his dreads out of his face.

I paused my stride long enough to shoot him a deadly glare before continuing to walk away. "I'm out."

"Yo, hold up. Where are you going?"

"I'm leaving. I'm not marryin' no jawn I don't know. I don't give a fuck what Pa says."

"You know how this shit goes, Kas. This is how it's been, long before either of our asses were born and long after we turn back to dust. Our families make alliances for wealth and power and strength. And if this helps our family, then you gotta suck it up and do what you gotta do, just like how Koda would've."

My eyes cut into his like daggers. "I'm not Koda. Why the fuck don't nobody seem to understand that shit?" I barked.

"I'm not sayin—"

I shook my head. "Nah. There are thousands of better ways, money being one of them, Mil. You and I both know that will take us so much further than me signing my name on a fuckin' piece of paper will."

Kamil ran his hand down his freshly groomed goatee before speaking up again. "Well, you can't pay your way out of this one, so you might as well throw some water on your face and get your fuckin' head in the game, nigga. Once Pa makes his decisions, they are always final."

I clenched my jaw tight. He was right, but I still didn't give a fuck. My father's mood had quickly made my already shit-filled day even shittier. I wasn't in the right headspace to entertain the idea of becoming a married man in six months. All I cared about was getting out of there. I'd deal with my father's bullshit later. I either needed a hard drink, a blunt, or to kill someone... maybe even all three. On my way out, I caught a glimpse of Cena standing a couple of feet away from my escape door.

She gave me a doe-eyed stare before casting her eyes to the LV initials etched into the jet-black leather purse hanging off her delicate wrist. From her naturally long hair that cascaded past her bra strap to her blemish-free, smooth caramel skin, she was beautiful, but I was too mad to care. Jrue was the only woman I was interested in getting to know, and an arranged marriage I had no say in wouldn't stop me from doing it.

Five

YARA ALVAREZ

"MMM. You like the way that dick feels against that pussy, baby?" Nate groaned while stroking his hard-on via video chat.

I licked my fingertips before stroking and flicking my clit harder. "Mmm. You feel so good, baby. Fill me up even deeper." I moaned while reaching into my nightstand to pull out my rose toy.

I spread my legs wide and pressed the vibrating toy to my clit and instantly began to moan louder.

"Use your fingers, baby. You know I don't like all those toys and shit," he complained, instantly killing my vibe.

I tossed my rose to the side and stroked my pussy in a daze. I loved Nate, but the phone sex had stopped cutting it for me months ago. Watching him hammer away at his oiled-up dick a few nights a week was old, and sending sexy videos had lost its touch.

Nate and I dated all throughout high school. At eighteen was the first time we'd separated in four years. I went off to college, and he enlisted in the navy. He'd been deployed four times since then, and it wasn't until three years ago that things between us rekindled when he came back into town, and we ended up getting back together. Fast forward to his current tour; he'd already been at sea for nine and a half months. The lonely nights and missed holidays weren't what I signed up for, but I loved who I loved, so I tolerated it. Besides, it wasn't like I was alone. I had my best friend and roommate, Jrue, to keep me company. And when she wasn't around, I enjoyed my time and space to do my own thing.

I zoned back into our phone sex session when I heard him groan in pleasure just before he erupted like a creamy volcano. His stomach glistened with nut as he panted. "Mmm, shit. Did you cum, baby?"

"Yeah. Like twice." I lied with a smile.

"Good."

"I'm gonna go take a shower, okay, baby? I'll talk to you tomorrow. I love you," I stated, hovering my thumb over the X button just before I heard him mutter.

"Okay. I love y—"

"Oops." I groaned with a sigh.

Nate came with his share of rules and boundaries, especially regarding sex. He disapproved of sex toys in the bedroom and was only okay with me using one since he was away. And even then, I couldn't do it on camera. And don't get me started on anal. The thought of ass play repulsed him. He wouldn't even dare stick a finger inside my booty when he would hit it from behind. With Nate, I knew how the next forty years of my life would go. Those reasons alone were enough for me to have a sneaky link while he was away serving our country. I saw it as a form of self-care by getting all the freak hoe out of my system while I could. Lord knows once I was married one day, it would be boring ass missionary for the rest of my natural-born days. Frustrated with the thought, I swiped over to my messages and sent a quick text to my side piece who was both wild and adventurous, two things Nate wasn't.

Me: *Wyd?*

Link: *Thinkin' bout you.*

Me: *Me on your mind is always a good thing.*

Link: *Come over and ride this face.*

Me: *Say less.*

CANAAN MCQUEEN

I SANG ALONGSIDE FUTURE, crooning away to his song, *"Love You Better,"* as I hit the interstate.

Future's voice dragged through my speakers as the bass vibrated the windows of my S-Class Mercedes. I had a long drive ahead of me to Rhode Island, so I lit a fresh blunt, cracked the sunroof, and got in my zone. The music faded when my father called. A cloud of thick smoke expelled from my nose before I pressed accept.

"What's up, Pop?" I answered.

Instead of hearing his voice on the other line, forceful hacking came through my car speakers. I frowned. "Pop? You good?" The line fell silent for a few seconds. "H-hello? Pop? You there?"

"I'm here," he finally answered.

"You good?"

"I'm fine."

"What's up?"

"We got word on the hit that took out Donovan the night of Kamil Barnes's bachelor party."

"Was I right?" I quizzed.

"Yeah. You were. It was the Simms family."

As a part of *The Order*, our family supplied others with drugs across the state and to the families in the tri-state area. As our biggest drug competitor, the Simms family had been a rival of *The Order* for years. They wanted our territories and our spot in *The Order*, which we all knew would never happen. Donovan's death still didn't sit right with me. It was senseless. They wanted smoke with the wrong ones. Had I been there that night when shit went down, things would've gone real fuckin' different.

"I fuckin' told you, Pop! I knew they were gonna make a fuckin' move."

"Me too."

"What do you need me to do? I'm ready to put a bullet in whoever for Donovan," I assured him.

"And Koda Barnes. Don't forget; he was supposed to marry your sister."

I sucked my teeth while shaking my head at everything that had gone down. "Yeah. Him too."

My eyes flashed wide when I saw Julius Barnes's name on my screen. "Hey, Pop. Let me call you back," I stated before clicking over to accept his call. "Boss, what can I do for you?"

"I'm growing impatient with your father, Canaan. He's yet to respond to my offer. Were you able to speak to him after our last conversation?"

I shifted uncomfortably before bobbing my head. "Yeah, I spoke to him briefly."

"And? I don't need to remind you of what you stand to gain if this deal goes through, do I?"

A quick no jerked my head. "No."

Julius wanted to expand his business dealings into our part of the state, but my father had no interest in allowing him to do that. He felt that each family in *The Order* had their own territories and business dealings for a reason, and the amount of territory Julius requested access to would give him majority control over the entire state. Although we had something he needed, he had something I needed too, even more, *power*. I was Silas McQueen's only son and heir to everything. But it didn't mean shit while he was still alive. Once I took over, I would have no problem giving Julius what he wanted, because the astronomical payout that came with it was worth it.

"Listen, we both know he's tired. I'm practically running the day-to-day stuff as is. Just give me more time to get him onboard with this."

"And what about your sister?"

I scoffed. "What about her?"

"Nothing. I'll be in touch," he said before the line went dead.

WHEN I ARRIVED at my destination, dozens of kids were laughing and yelling in the backyard. Once inside, I added my gift to the top of the tower of brightly wrapped birthday presents.

"You're late." Trinity scolded me with a frown across her honey-brown face.

One look at the scowl on her face, and I could tell she would've had her arms folded across her chest if it hadn't been for the Paw Patrol sheet cake occupying her hands.

"Looks to me like I'm right on time," I said, swiping a bit of icing from the side of the cake and sucking it off my finger.

"Ew, nigga! Get away from the cake!"

"Where's Za?"

"Follow me. We're about to sing Happy Birthday."

I followed behind Trinity, admiring how her hips swayed and her ass sat up in the jeans painted on her body. I licked my lips, tempted to steal her away for a chance to dip inside her, but a familiar, miniature voice captured my attention.

"Daddy! Daddy! Daddy!" Zahir screamed as he fell into my arms and wrapped his tiny arms around my neck.

I scooped him up into a tight hug. "Hey, birthday boy! How's Daddy's big man doing today?"

"Good! I'm happy you came!"

"I told you I would," I stated, adjusting the strap of the party hat around his chin.

"I missed you."

I rubbed his back. "Daddy missed you too, but don't worry. We won't be apart forever," I promised him.

"Are you ready for us to sing Happy Birthday so you can blow out your candles?" Trinity asked him.

"Yeah!"

Zahir jumped out of my arms and took his seat at the head of the table so that his friends and family could sing to him. Everyone cheered as he blew out his candles. For the past four years, Trinity and Zahir had been two of my best-kept secrets. When I met her, she was a stripper in New York. We only fucked around a couple of times before she told me she was pregnant. I fought against it for nine months, unwilling to claim a baby from a jawn I ain't know shit about. It wasn't until the probability of paternity came back at 99.999 percent, I had to accept it and blessed my son with my last name. After that, I moved her and the baby out of New York to a spot in Rhode Island for protection. There was no way my family could find out that I'd had a baby with a stripper, at least not until I took over for my father. Instead of accepting them, I knew my family would see them as trash, and I would be labeled even more irresponsible than they already thought I was. I gave her money each month, and whenever I came out to do business with the Palmers, I pulled up on them and stayed a couple of days before returning to Philly.

After watching him open his presents, I leaned against the refrigerator watching Trinity clean up around the kitchen. "The least you could do is help me clean up instead of standing over there stuffing your face with cake," she griped.

I savored the last bite of sweet icing before pulling a roll of hundred-dollar bills out of my pocket and putting it on the kitchen counter. "There you go. That's for you. You happy now?"

She smacked her teeth. "You think that's supposed to make up for everything you miss out on around here?"

"I'm doing the best I fuckin' can, aight?"

"Do better!" She yelled, curls spilling over her face.

"Whoa. Lower your voice, aight? You know what it is and what I'm working toward for us. I'm doing what I gotta do, and I need you to be patient."

She threw her head back to avoid tears from rolling down her face. "I've been patient for too long, and I'm tired."

My brow creased. "What are you saying?"

"I'm saying my bed is cold, Canaan," she declared while brushing some of the confetti off the kitchen counter.

I shrugged. "I'm here now."

"For how long, huh? You were supposed to be here yesterday to help me set up for Za's party today, and yet you still get to come in here and play Superman because he sees you at a minimum twice a fucking month!" she vented.

I knew she was angry, stressed, and downright tired. The money was cool, pacifying even, but it wasn't enough, not to her. Until I could secure the spot as the head of my family, she would have to accept my apologies a little while longer. I almost had everything I ever wanted in reach.

"I'm sorry."

"You're always sorry."

"I'm trying."

"Yeah, me too," she scoffed.

I walked up behind her and wrapped my arms around her waist. "Things are going to change, T. Just keep holding me down a little longer." I encouraged her with a kiss against the red tattoo ink on the side of her neck.

Seven

KAS

THURSDAY ROLLED AROUND, and the minutes of the day ticked by slowly as I waited to see Jrue. I couldn't wait to see what ideas she'd come up with. I had my assistant reach out with minimal details, just a time and location. She likely had no idea what she was walking into. Plus, I was curious to see how she handled herself in a five-star restaurant, let alone the most exclusive five-star restaurant in Philly, Savor Soul. It was the only spot in the state with a live pianist in the elegant dining room, a carefully curated menu of upscale takes, and one of the most impressive wine lists on the east coast. I sauntered into the building wearing Dior on my back and Ferragamo loafers on my feet when my phone rang.

"Kamil, I can't talk right now," I answered.

"You've been dodging my calls for days."

"Yeah, well, I've been busy."

"Your ass should've stuck around a little longer the other night."

I smacked my lips. "For what?"

"Your ass would've learned something."

"You gon' tell me, or you gon' keep on with the riddles and shit?"

"I was going over the books, making sure we received payouts for every location in our territory this month."

"And?"

"And, I happened to come across a weird transaction under an alias business. I did some research and traced it back and found out that Pa's been sending Silas McQueen money for *years*, and it kicked up more in the years after his wife died."

"How much?"

"That's the thing; they are all these random lump sums with no memos attached to them or anything. It's the weirdest paper trail ever."

My brows heightened. "Why the hell would he be sending Silas McQueen money?"

"That's what I don't know."

"Keep digging and let me know what you find. I gotta go. I'll call you later."

"Aight, bet."

I ended the call and made my way to one of the best tables in the house. Once seated, I waited for Jrue to arrive. I tore my eyes around the dimly lit restaurant, taking in the purple, pink, and golden hues of the sunset through the floor-to-ceiling glass walls that offered unmatched views of the city from every seat in the house.

"Savor Soul? I'm impressed." Jrue announced herself as she approached the table.

I studied her from head to toe, admiring how her voluminous curls bounced when she walked. She wore a caramel-colored blouse, brown pleated parachute pants, and strappy heels that showed off her white toes.

I stood to greet her while she took her seat. "Oh yeah?"

"Yeah. How'd you manage to snag a table here?"

"Easy. I own the place."

"W-what? Are you serious? It's beautiful here. It was like everything was handpicked."

"It was, down to the food. I wanted a carefully curated menu of upscale takes on traditional soul food dishes. Have you eaten here before?"

"Can't say I have, but I've only heard good things."

"Well, you're in for a treat."

"I'm sure."

"You changed your hair," I commented, switching subjects.

"Yeah. The twists had to go. Figured I'd rock my natural hair for a while," she said, tossing her dark curls over her shoulder. One look at her beautiful face and I knew she was nervous. She didn't look as on her game as she was the last time we'd crossed each other's paths. I figured it was best to ease her into the business part of the meeting, and we'd have our pleasure first.

"What are you drinking?"

"I thought this was a business meeting."

"I'm a busy man, Jrue. That means I sometimes have to work through my lunches and dinners. With that being said, I like to have a little pleasure with my business, so what is it you said to me before, when in Rome?"

She chuckled. "Yeah, okay then. In that case, I'll have a tequila sunrise."

"Okay."

AFTER WE FINISHED dinner and a couple of drinks, I decided it was time to switch gears. "Now that we've had our pleasure, let's get down to business," I insisted.

"Of course," she said, digging in her bag and pulling out a manilla folder. "For starters, I put together a mood board for you."

She handed me the folder with a single piece of paper with different images and a warm color palette before speaking up again. "You said you wanted sexy, right? So I'm thinking crushed velvet and cashmere as our two focal textures for furniture and maybe even some custom art pieces or textured sculptures. It's sexy and comfortable, which are two things you want to feel when you're in the privacy of your own home, right? Plus, you said these are luxury condos, and cashmere is an exquisite texture."

My forehead creased. "What the fuck is this?"

She looked as if she was begging for a hole in the floor to appear and swallow her whole. "Excuse me?"

"You heard me. What the fuck is this?"

"Do you not understand what a mood board is, or were you looking for something different?"

"I understand what a mood board is just fine; I just thought you'd do better."

She frowned. "Um, wow. Okay, I'm sorry I've disappointed you. I can go back to the drawing board and get you something different. The more feedback and direction you give me, the better my ideas will be. I mean, what would be great is if I could see the space and get a feel for how I can utilize it, or you can just tell me how you want it to feel, Kas."

"I already told you I want it to be sexy."

"What's sexy to you?"

You, I thought, but instead, I let out an exasperated huff and said, "Listen, Jrue. I think what you're trying to do is cool and shit, but it's not me, and it's not the look I envisioned for my condos, especially not in the final stretch. I look at everyone I choose to work with as an investment, and I'm not in the mood to lose a great deal of money on a bad one."

"And now you listen, Kas. I know how to balance color, and I'm super creative. I—I just got caught up in my head. If you just give me another chance, I can do better. I promise you I can make this come together. I just need another twenty-four hours to let my creative juices flow. Give me that, and I'll prove it to you."

I couldn't decide which was sexier, her determination or how the word juices fell off her tongue. "Fine," I agreed, "another twenty-four hours."

Eight

JRUE

I SAT across from Kas feeling more exposed than if I'd been completely naked in front of him. His harsh criticism of my designs ripped through me as if I were a thin piece of film. As grateful as I was for a second chance, I was beginning to hate his *sexy ass*. By the time I got home, I was still in my feelings. I'd delivered what he'd asked for, and it was clear he was resistant to suggestions or change. He struck me as someone who may never be satisfied. With a glass of wine in my hand, I paced back and forth across my living room carpet.

"You got this, Jrue. You got this. He threw you off your game once. You ain't gon' let that shit happen again." I coached myself before sitting down at my laptop to come up with a different concept to present to Kas. I didn't care if I had to pull an all-nighter. I wasn't about to let him knock me off my square twice.

"And send," I mumbled after emailing him my updated pitch in ten of the twenty-four hours he'd given me.

With one eye open, I sluggishly made my way to my bedroom and fell across my queen-sized bed. Just before I drifted off, I heard my phone chime. I rolled over and felt around on my nightstand for my phone. My eyes popped wide when I saw a reply from Kas at 5:27 a.m.

Better. Dinner tonight at eight for your in-person pitch. My assistant will be in touch with the details.

I locked my phone without replying. "Motherfuck." I groaned, excited and frazzled all at once.

I WALKED into the restaurant later that evening, fifteen minutes early and ready for whatever he planned to throw my way. Although I had my game face on, my nerves were on a thousand. I could smell the alluring scent of his expensive cologne before he even approached the table.

"Hey. You're early," he stated.

I twisted my neck in his direction, eyes following him as he took his seat across from me. "Yeah. Thanks for, um, giving me a second chance."

Kas adjusted his tie. "This will be your last. Go ahead. The floor is yours."

His cold tone struck a chord, causing me to clear my throat. *He's not going to knock you off your square. He's not going to knock you off your square*, I repeated to myself.

"I've been studying you since we met. First, the night at the club. Then again at the cafe and even last night at the restaurant."

"And what have you learned?" he asked, intrigued.

"Well, for one, you're confident. Polished. And from what I can tell, a minimalist."

"A minimalist, huh?"

"Yes. On top of those things, you're also the face behind this real estate venture. Last night during our meeting, you said you want your condos to be a vibe. The revised design proposal I sent you is a good blend of masculinity and femininity. It's sexy and high-class, yet low-key, just like the people who are going to live in your condos," I stated, pulling out hard copies of my proposal.

He looked over it, flipping through the papers in front of him. "Hmm."

"Do you have any questions or comments?"

"I like the idea of subtle hints of gold in the marble flooring."

"Good. Anything else I can answer?"

"There's that crushed velvet and cashmere again. You won't let it go, will you?"

"Nope."

"Why not leather? Leather is sexy."

"Leather is too masculine and cold. The combination I picked is going to be epic, trust me."

"Mmm," he grumbled. "What makes you think that?"

"It's not what I think; it's what I know," I assured him.

There was a pregnant pause before he spoke up again. "I like it."

"You do?" I quizzed, prepped, and ready for his rebuttals.

"Yeah. You were a lot more confident this time."

Lines pulled at the corners of my mouth. "Well, thanks."

"I'll have my assistant draw up the contract and send over everything first thing in the morning. Sound good?"

My chin plunged in agreement. "That sounds great. Off hand, do you know what my budget will be for the project?"

Kas tore his eyes down to the table while smirking. "As the lead designer on the project, you'll have full creative control, and as far as your budget goes, whatever you need, you can have."

If I could've, I would've done a backflip on top of the bar right then and there. I'd finally locked in with the type of clientele I'd been searching for to take my business to the next level.

"So, when do I get to see the space?"

"When do you want to?"

"As soon as possible. I'd love to finalize some of these ideas once I see what I'm working with."

"I'll have my assistant arrange all of that later. Right now, it's time to celebrate," he said, waving down the waiter.

Once we had a fresh bottle of champagne in front of us, Kas filled our glasses and extended his in the air. "To new business ventures."

Our glasses clinked. "To new business ventures."

Nine

KAS

BY THE END OF DINNER, Jrue and I were still grinning from ear to ear. I wasn't ready to leave her presence, so instead of waiting for my assistant to get her access to the site, I decided to take her myself.

"So, do you have plans after this?"

She let out a soft chuckle. "I picked up a shift at Bliss, so I've got to be at the club in a few hours. Until then, no big plans. You?"

I took a sip from my drink before responding. "I'd like to show you the site if you're up for it. Not sure you have on the right shoes."

Jrue flashed her bright smile at me. "You underestimate me. I've got a pair of knock-around sneakers in my trunk. I'll be fine."

I loved a woman who was prepared. "Okay, bet. Let's go."

Once Jrue retrieved her shoes from her car, she ducked inside mine, and I whizzed us a few miles away to the building site.

I SHOWED her around the forty-two-story building. The Olympic-sized pool, state-of-the-art gym and equipment, rooftop bar, and firepits equipped it with all the amenities anyone could ever ask for. Over seventy-five percent of the building was complete already. All that was missing was a taste of me.

"Are you excited?" I asked as she snapped pictures with her phone during our tour.

"Very. My mind is bubbling over with ideas right now. It's such a gorgeous space."

We continued to trek across the lightly sanded wood floors inside the three-bedroom condo. "Good. I can't wait to see what you do with it."

"I'm thinking maybe a textured accent wall to bring their eyes to the beautiful view of the city. Oh, and maybe a chaise over there in the corner with a cashmere throw pillow."

"I want minimal furniture in the master so that you can get a feel for how big and luxurious the space is," I commented.

"See. I told you I already peeped you were a minimalist."

"I guess you're right."

I leaned my shoulder against the wall, watching as Jrue explored the space solo. I could hear her mumbling throughout while her cell camera clicked.

"You think you can work with the space?" I asked when she returned.

"Come to the bedroom with me," she beckoned.

I followed her down the hallway, stopping in the doorframe as she made her way to the middle of the empty room.

"Come stand next to me and close your eyes."

Once I was standing next to her, I peered down at her five-foot-five frame. "Do I really need to close my eyes?"

"Yes. It's mandatory," she stated with a coy smile.

I rolled my eyes before slamming them shut. "Fine."

"Alright. Now tell me if you can picture it. A nice, California king-sized bed against the far wall with a plush rug underneath to account for the cold marble floors in the winter. Because you know, Philly winters will have you feelin' like you're near death. Can you see it?"

I tipped my head forward. "Yeah."

"Alright. Now let's add an oversized velvet throw across the foot of the bed for comfort. And pillows. Lots and lots of pillows. Nothing screams comfort like pillows."

"What do I find when I pull back the sheets?"

"Silk. Cream or brown," she answered without hesitation.

I slid a smirk up one-half of my face. "Nice."

"That's all I have for now off the top of my head, but I'll have more by the end of the night."

I slowly opened my eyes to see her staring up at me. We stared at each other, stealing a few seconds of silence before I spoke up. "Although much of your work will be concentrated on the twentieth floor and the common areas on the first floor, I'll make sure you have access to the entire building. All but the penthouse level," I confirmed.

"Why not? What's up there? Your secret sex room or something?" she joked.

I smirked at her comment. Had she known what I used the penthouse apartment for, smiling would be the furthest thing from her mind. The whole level had soundproof walls throughout and tinted floor-to-ceiling windows. Black tarps covered every square inch of the floor for quick cleanups when business dealings went south.

"Does the thought of something like that intrigue you?" I inquired.

"Relax. I was only kidding."

"Give me your phone."

She hesitated for a split second before handing it to me. "What do you need it for?"

"I'm putting my number in it so you can contact me if you need me."

"With questions about the project, right?"

I shot my eyes up at her. "Right."

"Thanks again for the tour."

I bowed my head. "As I said at dinner, I'll have my assistant draw up the paperwork and send it to you in the morning. Once everything is signed, I'll wire over half the funds, and you can begin."

"That sounds good. Thanks. You won't be disappointed!" She assured me with a warm smile.

My eyes hung on her lips as I slid my tongue across my own. "I'm sure I won't be."

Ten

JRUE

"HAPPY BIRTHDAY TO YOU. *Happy birthday to you. Happy birthday, dear Yara. Happy birthday to you!*" I sang alongside her cousin and a few other family members and co-workers. A smile jotted across Yara's lips as we sang and cheered, then she leaned in to blow out the long, gold birthday candle in the slice of strawberry cheesecake in front of her.

"Yay! Thank you so much for coming out and having a drink with me! Now, if I don't see a drink in everyone's hand, there's going to be a problem!" she announced with a dawning smile.

"I'll be right back," I declared, sliding away from the cocktail table.

"Where you going?"

"Bathroom."

"Wait! Let me come too. Those three shots I had are already ready to come out!" Yara hooked her arm in mine as we made our way through the bar to the bathrooms. "Thanks for putting all this together for me, Jrue. You're the best."

I shook my head. "It's no problem. It's your birthday. Everyone deserves to have at least one non-shitty day out of the year."

"Amen to that. Our twenties are hard enough as is."

"Exactly. You heard from Nate today?"

She huffed. "I woke up to a birthday text this morning. And it'll probably be like it was last year—me having to save a piece of cake and blow out my candle in front of him while he sings the Black version of Happy Birthday."

"Aww, that's cute."

Her lean shoulders rose and fell. "Yeah, I guess. It's just old," she expressed before we stepped into separate stalls to relieve our bladders.

"Because he's away?"

Yara continued to vent over her stream of pee. "Especially because he's away. I don't know. I need some spice in my life... something to shake up the norm. I feel like I'm just coasting along in this relationship with nothing new to look forward to."

"At least you have someone willing to celebrate you, even from halfway around the world," I reminded her.

Before applying soap, she met me at the sink and wet her hands underneath the automatic faucet. "So, what you're saying is, I'm a selfish bitch."

"No. I'm not saying that at all. I'm just trying to do my job as your best friend and help you look on the bright side of shit."

"Am I wrong for wanting something different? Something to look forward to outside of the daily?"

"No."

"How would you feel if you were in my shoes?"

I tossed the crumpled paper towel into the trash. "I don't know. Maybe what you have would be enough for me, maybe it wouldn't. I would have to be in a long-distance relationship to answer that, or a relationship at all."

"Remind me again why you refuse to let anyone wife you?"

"You talk as if I have a sign tatted on my forehead that says nigga repellant."

"I mean..."

My eyes rolled skyward. "Whatever. Maybe I had this fairytale all built out in my head at one point or another. But now, I'm not looking for love, and it's not looking for me," I announced as we made our way out of the bathroom.

"I'm not saying you have to run out and make forty different dating profiles, but don't close off your heart to the possibility of things. You're too good of a person to be alone for the rest of your life."

Seconds after we returned to the table, I spotted her boyfriend, Nate, heading toward us in uniform with a bouquet of long-stem red roses cradled in his arm. My brows arched high. "Oh shit."

"What?"

Yara spun around, and her eyes caught his. "Nate? Oh my God! What are you doing here?"

"It's your birthday, babe. I couldn't miss it two years in a row."

Her eyes began to mist with happy tears. "Are you for real right now? Is this real?"

"Yup. I'm here, baby," he assured her before placing the flowers in her hand.

"F-for how long?" she quizzed, her brown orbs still wide with shock.

"For a few days, then I've got to stay on base for evaluation and everything for another few weeks or so, and then I'm back again for good for a while. But don't worry; the base is only about a two-hour drive from here," he assured her.

"This is crazy."

"Crazier than this?" he asked.

Everyone's eyes widened when he slid a ring box out of his pocket and got down on one knee. Yara clasped her freshly manicured nails over her mouth as tears welled up in her eyes. "Oh my God, baby! Are you serious?"

"Yara Alvarez, I love you with every breath in me. Will you marry me?"

Nate popped the diamond out of the box and slid it on her finger. "Oh my—oh my God!"

"Is that a yes?"

"Yes! Yes! It's a yes!" Yara squealed before enveloping him in a tight hug.

The bar erupted with whistles and cheers of joy before friends and strangers bombarded them with congratulatory comments. I kept a smile leaning on half of my mouth, but truthfully, my cheeks felt like sandbags. It had been almost two years since I lost my first love. I hadn't been interested in falling for anyone ever since. I didn't know why allowing myself to get close to anyone still felt like a betrayal, but it did.

Nevertheless, Yara's surprise engagement was a bittersweet moment for me. On one hand, I was overjoyed for her. She was my best friend, after all. But there was a part of me that wondered if I would ever have that or if I would ever be able to open my heart to anyone like that again. Loving a man was one of the most dangerous things a woman could do, and as happy as Yara looked, I didn't know if I was willing to take that risk again.

A YEAR *and nine months ago.*

The roads were slick from the rain. My boyfriend, Darius, was behind the wheel, driving us back to my apartment. I watched his wipers violently swiping back and forth across the windshield, wicking away the moisture. The light changed, and the car stopped, causing me to steal a glance at him. He had a head full of waves, warm cinnamon-brown skin, and eyes I always found myself getting lost in.

"Why you lookin' at me like that?" he asked, side-eyeing me.

"What? I can't look at you now? You shy, bae?" I giggled.

He smirked, revealing a glimpse of his teeth. They were white with a gap between the front two teeth. I liked it. I remember always trying to slide my tongue through it when we fucked.

"Nah, for real. You good?"

I nodded. "I'm great. Belly full, and I still have leftovers for later," I stated while tearing my eyes down to the warm to-go box cradled in my lap.

The light changed, and he pressed the gas while placing his hand on my thigh. "I hope you got room in that belly for me."

"Always."

Darius and I had been together for almost nine months. It was my longest and healthiest relationship to date. I'd known I'd loved him since the sixth month but had still held out on saying it up until now. Now, it was bubbling up from my heart and sitting on the tip of my tongue.

"Bae," I started, somewhat breathless.

"Yeah?"

"There's something I wanna tell you."

"What is it? Oh, wait. Hold up; this my cousin Jassir calling," he acknowledged before answering his phone. "Yeah? What? Right now? Aight, I'm dropping Jrue off now. Text me where you at, and I'll be on my way in a minute."

Darius hung up the phone with a sigh. "Everything alright?" I asked.

"Yeah. That nigga car broke down, and he needs me to scoop him. So, I'ma drop you off, get up with him, and then make my way back to you so we can finish our date."

I huffed. "He can't call nobody else?"

"Nah. You know how that nigga is. Besides, that's family. Don't worry. I won't be out all night. I'll be right back."

"Fine, okay."

Darius pulled up in front of my building. "Hold up. Tell me what you were gonna tell me before he called."

I shook my head. "It can wait until you get back."

"You sure?"

I shot him a reassuring smile. "Yeah."

"Aight, then. I'll hit you when I'm on my way."

I pecked his soft lips. "Okay. Be safe."

"I'm always safe, girl," he replied with a sincere smirk.

I kissed his warm lips once more before hopping out and making my way inside. Two hours passed without a word from him. I'd been calling and texting without response since the first hour. It wasn't until three o'clock the following day that I got a phone call from his mother telling me that he and Jassir had been involved in a drive-by robbery and were both shot to death at a red light. My first love had died without knowing I loved him. I couldn't stomach the idea of ever loving someone again.

YARA SNAPPED her fingers in front of my eyes. "Um, helllooooooo? Earth to Jrue. Are you there?"

"What? Oh. I'm sorry."

"Where'd you go just now? You were staring off into the abyss!"

I shook my head. "It's nothing. I'm sorry. I'm here. I'm right here! And oh my God! Let me see the ring!"

She dipped her hand in front of my face, allowing me to examine the princess-cut diamond on her ring finger. "Oh my God! It's beautiful!"

"I know!" She squealed. "He did such a good job! Did you know about this?"

I swung my head in a no. "No. I knew nothing. Nothing at all. He kept this quiet as kept."

"Are you lying to me right now?"

"I mean, he may have asked my thought or two on the ring, but I didn't know when he was going to do it!"

She smacked my arm. "But you did know something was up! Way to keep a secret, bestie!"

"You're welcome!"

"Do you mind if we skate off a little early and, uh, y'know, celebrate?" She winked.

"No. Go right ahead. I'll see you back at the apartment later. Or not." I smirked.

"Before I go, let's take one more shot!" Yara insisted.

"One more shot? No. I'm good," I declared, head wagging from side to side.

"C'mon, it's my birthday! Pleaseeeeee?" she whined.

"Okay, okay. Fine!"

Nate ordered another round for us before her cousin made a toast. "To the future Mr. and Mrs. Williams."

"Cheers!"

Eleven

YARA

NATE WAS GONE AGAIN, and I couldn't have been more relieved. I had a lot of new feelings to sort through, and I couldn't do it with him lying up underneath me. We had the rest of our lives for shit like that. I should've been happy to be engaged to a man who loved me, but every time I looked down at his ring and saw it glitter with every tiny move I made, I felt sick. I'd been complaining to the universe about the lack of change in my life and had somehow manifested a proposal from the only man I ever loved. I should've been ecstatic. Over the moon, even. But my feelings were far from that. I'd had my dream wedding planned out since I was fourteen, and now that the opportunity had presented itself in full-force, I felt like a pretty little bird that would never fully be able to fly free.

I made my living planning other people's happily ever afters, but for some reason, I had no interest in thinking about the best day of my life, let alone planning it. Regardless of my feelings, I knew I needed to do the right thing and break things off with my fling, so when he called me over to his place, I saw it as the perfect opportunity to do so.

He pulled me inside by my waist the minute he opened the door. Once inside, he placed a sloppy kiss against my lips before I pushed him off. "I didn't come here for that."

I put some space between us before casting my eyes on him. The day we met, I knew Canaan was dangerous and full of too much power. And yet, I *had* to fuck around and find out for myself. He was over six feet tall, built, and to my surprise, he was just as dominant as he was gentle in the bedroom. He'd been my best-kept, caramel brown secret for a few months, but we both knew we were on borrowed time.

"Then what did you come here for?"

"To talk."

"We don't talk."

"I know, but this happened recently, so I think it's only right that we do," I told him while showing him my ring finger.

He batted his long lashes at the diamond and scoffed, causing me to arch a questioning eyebrow in his direction. "What was that sound about?"

"Nothing. Congrats."

"Tell me."

Canaan blew the air out of his cheeks while scrunching his wide nostrils. "You not ready for this. You and I both know that."

I folded my arms across my chest. "What makes you so sure?"

"Because you're having too much fun with me, Yara. Tell me you're not."

"I am, but that's not the point."

"That's exactly the point. One look at you, and I can tell you don't know how you even feel about wearing that nigga childish ass ring."

My eyes clouded with tears, and I quickly rolled them skyward to keep them from falling. "That's none of your business."

"Oh, so you're good with it then?"

I gave a one-shoulder shrug. "I'm still trying to figure this shit out, okay?"

"And you thought you'd do it here? With your legs aimed toward my ceiling?"

I shook my head. "I told you, that's not why I came here!"

"Then what did you come here for? For me to talk you out of it?" he asked, sweeping his hand down his freshly lined goatee.

"No! Not at all. I know exactly what this is between us, and now I'm cutting things off like an adult instead of just ghosting your ass, but now you got me thinkin' I should've."

"Yeah, well, as long as you know what's up."

"You're an arrogant mothafucka, and I'm glad to be done with you! I swear I don't even know why I wasted my time coming here in the first place!"

"You came here to tell me you ain't want this dick no more, and you can't even bring yourself to say it!" he barked, drawing closer to me.

I put my hand out to stop him, but he swatted it away with ease. "Canaan—"

"Oh, nah, Yara, baby. You gon' have to tell me to stop. You gon' have to tell me you don't want me to bend you over this couch right now and fuck the shit outta that pussy."

I sighed. He'd been bending me over and breaking my back for four months. We didn't focus on too much conversation outside of the bedroom. When we met, we agreed on a casual, no strings attached connection. He'd never been to my spot nor knew what part of the city I stayed in. We either met up at his place or did our dirt in five-star hotels around the city. He knew what I wanted him to know about my relationship with Nate, and I didn't nag him about who he was with as long as things between us stayed clean. As badly as I wanted to quit him, he was right. I couldn't bring myself to say the words.

"I—"

The hungry look in Canaan's hickory brown eyes snatched the oxygen from my lungs before he cut me off with a kiss. "Let me show you just how not ready you are to give all this up." He whispered while resting his stiff dick against my thigh.

My fingertips skated down his bulging chestnut muscles. I knew my attraction to him would be my undoing, but the tingling feeling in my panties left me vulnerable to his advances. And without anyone here to save me from myself or to stop my pussy from leaking at the sight of him, I slipped right back into the lion's den.

"This is the last time, okay?" I whispered against his sultry lips.

A ghost of a smile crossed his lips as he slid his bottom lip between his polished white teeth. "Yeah, okay."

Canaan's dark-eyed gaze tugged at my heartstrings, unraveling me more and more by the second. He was as tempting as the snake in the Garden of Eden. His soft lips consumed mine once more while his thumbs skated across my pierced nipples. My eyes fell to his dick, watching the veins pop out as he stroked himself. He offered the type of dick I liked. The kind that made my toes curl with no feelings involved. I knew we were both keeping secrets, and I didn't give a fuck. I'd have to figure out another way to quit him; consequences be damned.

Twelve

KAS

CANAAN MCQUEEN COULDN'T BE TRUSTED. I'd known that all my life, yet I sat across the room from him with his sister, Cena, by my side. I hadn't tried to reach out to her until days after the announcement of our marriage hit *The Order*. As much as I was against the entire thing, I figured it would only be right to have her as my date to Kamil's wedding since all the families in *The Order* would be in attendance.

"Yo, the photographer wants to get a few more pictures of us," Kamil announced, nudging me with his elbow.

I bowed my head once and cleared my throat before standing up and running my palms down my crisp, onyx black tux. Kamil and I stepped off to smile and pose for the wedding photos I knew they'd spent thousands of dollars to have captured.

"Love looks good on you, blood. Congratulations." I dapped him up before pulling him into a quick embrace.

He cheesed. "Thank you. Thank you. I only wish Koda could've been here to see it."

I dipped my chin. "Yeah. Me too. How's it feel being a married man now?" I asked, changing the subject to keep the vibe light.

"Ain't no different. Shit, you gon' find out soon enough."

I rolled my eyes. "Don't start with that shit."

Kamil laughed. "Yeah, aight. Just wait and see."

It felt good to laugh and joke with my brother as the photographers continued to snap away until satisfied. I made my way through the sea of wedding guests to the bar to grab a drink before heading back over to join Cena.

"Yo, I'm out," Canaan announced when I approached the bar.

"You dippin' out early?"

"Yeah. I'ma change outta this shit and meet up with my boys at the club."

I gave him a farewell nod. "Aight, peace. Thanks for comin'."

He extended his hand to dap me up. "No problem."

I returned the gesture, knowing deep down I didn't trust him as far as I could throw him. In my eyes, he was bad for business and didn't hide the fact that he was itching to take over whenever the time came for his father to take his last breath. I pushed my opinion of him to the side when I approached Cena. She was draped in burgundy from head to toe, wearing a matching crop top and pencil skirt set that hugged her curves just right and stopped at her ankles. Four-inch burgundy heels were on her feet, showing off her white toes.

"I got you a glass of wine."

Cena flashed me a pasted-on smile before swiping her hair behind her right ear and accepting the glass. "Oh. Thanks."

"You havin' fun?" I asked.

She dipped her chin in a silent nod. "Yeah. I can't believe this will be us in a few months," she stated, trying her best to keep the conversation flowing.

"Yeah."

"Do you have any ideas or things you want or don't want?"

I shrugged. "To be honest, I never thought about it. Didn't see myself getting married."

"So soon?"

"Ever," I corrected her.

"Oh."

"Yeah..."

Silence hung between us. The longer it dragged on, the harder it became to begin again. I tore my eyes across the dance floor, zeroing in on the bride and groom. "They do look happy, though."

She twisted her neck to me and flashed a warmer, more genuine smile. "Yeah. They do."

"Is this what you always pictured for yourself?"

"What do you mean?"

"Am I what you see when you picture a husband? I mean, this isn't awkward for you? Y'know, losing Koda and having to—"

She held up her hand to stop me. "You want the truth?" she quizzed before taking a sip of the Moscato in her glass.

"Always."

"Then, no. You aren't. And as far as awkwardness, it's not like Koda and I knew much more about each other than you and I did. I'm sorry you had to lose your brother. Both sides lost people that night, so I'm doing what I have to do for my family, just like you."

I huffed. "There's gotta be another way that makes it so everyone can get what they want, right? Can you talk to your father?"

"You and I both know my father is a traditional man in every sense of the word. His mind is made up. You're better off just trying to look on the bright side of things like I do."

I took a swig of my drink before asking, "And what is the bright side in all of this?"

She shrugged her exposed shoulders. "Don't take this the wrong way. You're a handsome man. It's just..."

I cut her off. "You ain't gotta explain yourself to me. You shouldn't have to marry me if I'm not who you wanna be with. That's all I'm saying."

"You sound like you've already got your heart set on someone else."

The moment the words fell off her tongue, Jrue's face invaded my thoughts. I fluttered my head from left to right. "Nah. It's nothin' like that." I deflected.

Cena cocked her head to the side, studying me. "You were serious about never wanting to get married, huh?"

"Deadass."

"You were just unfortunate enough to be born into the wrong family. I guess we both were."

"Yeah."

"If it had to be any family, I guess I'm okay with it being yours. Because those Riveras are crazy as hell!" she joked.

We laughed in unison. "You're right about that. Hell, some of them Underwoods ain't wrapped too tight either," I mumbled, knowing the room was filled with them.

Cena and I continued our conversation, and I promised myself to focus on my money and my family. If it didn't have anything to do with that, I didn't have time for it. Besides, I had no time for distractions and no business falling in love.

Thirteen

JRUE

"I CAN MAKE *it hurricane on it. Hunnit bands, make it rain on it. Tie it up, put a chain on it. Make you tattoo my name on it.*" Chris Brown's voice bellowed through the speakers at Bliss.

I stood in a trance, watching the girls on stage twirl around their poles like ballerinas. It'd been days since I'd seen Kas, and I still couldn't peel my thoughts away from him. I'd been in a daze throughout the night, smiling for no reason as he danced through my head. Whenever asked, I played off my cheek-to-cheek grin as nothing but slapping on a smile to make money. After all, we *were* in a party atmosphere.

Amid the trap music that spilled from the club speakers, I made my way to the VIP section with two sparkling bottles of Moët atop my tray. I swaggered over to the table and placed the bottles in front of the trio of men with about half a dozen girls dancing in their section. "Anything else I can get you?" I yelled over the music to one of the guys.

"We can start with your number, gorgeous," he said, attempting to slide his hand in mine.

I pulled it away and let my eyes glaze over him. I'd peeped him occasionally stealing glimpses of me throughout the night, while he and his boys made their dollars rain over the strippers flocking to their section. He was over six feet tall, with a freshly groomed beard clinging to the lower half of his caramel face and diamonds in his earlobes that looked like they cost a month's rent each.

He was attractive, but the way he was lusting over me wasn't. His first mistake was assuming that just because I worked at a strip club, I'd be ready and willing to return his unwarranted sexual advances. Money flowing like the Mississippi was a typical thing at Bliss, and too many niggas tried to use it as bait. But the way my morals were set up, I would never allow myself to fall for their games. Kas was different. Although I'd met him inside these same walls, he was nothing like the ravenous patrons that frequented Bliss. He had manners and class.

"What's your name, beautiful?" he quizzed, tuning me back into the conversation.

"Jrue."

His pouty lips danced around a smile. I was minimally impressed. Not because it wasn't pleasant but because the only smile that I had on my mind belonged to Kasim Barnes. "I'm Canaan," he announced.

"Are you good on bottles for now, Canaan?" I asked, rephrasing my original question.

"Yeah. We good."

"Alright. I'll be back to check on you in a few." I turned to walk away when his nose caught my scent.

He gripped my arm to stop me from walking away. "What are you wearing?" he yelled over the music.

"Um, clothes."

"No. I mean, your fragrance. What perfume are you wearing? You smell good enough to eat."

I knew he was right. I smelled like a sweet mix of vanilla bourbon, wood, and jasmine. "Oh, uh, Valentino."

"Valentino, huh? I like it."

I flashed him a half smile out of courtesy. "Yeah, okay. Thanks." As I turned my back, I felt his sleazy ass cop a free handful of my ass. "Excuse you! This is a no-contact club. Don't touch me again," I warned. I didn't have a problem standing on my own two feet.

"My fault, *bitch*," he sneered, tossing his hands up in surrender.

"*Bitch*? Who you callin' a bitch?" I snapped.

I reacted quickly, flinging my tray against the table and sending the bottles he'd paid for crashing to the ground. He had me fucked up. I'd declined his weak ass advances, and he thought it was cool to grope me from behind. Enraged, I drew back my hand to smack him when Viper, the head security guard, snatched me back. Whip appeared from the shadows with a scowl across his aging face. He assessed the damage within seconds before directing his attention to the pussy nigga who'd put his hands on me to figure out what happened.

"Look at what that bitch did to my section! I want her ass fired!" Canaan demanded.

I lunged at him, but Viper's boulder-like arms kept me restrained with ease. "I got your bitch!"

He taunted me as Viper escorted me away from the scene, kicking and screaming. "Yeah. That's right! Get that hoe outta my section!"

Whip followed behind us, trying to do damage control. "What the fuck happened back there, Jrue? You can't fuckin' fight my patrons!" he scolded me.

"He put his fuckin' hands on me, Whip! What did you expect me to do?"

"Loosen the fuck up a bit! He was kidding. You know how niggas be when they get liquor in their system!"

I frowned as my body started to shake from rage. "Are you kidding me right now?"

"Listen, just go in the back and calm the fuck down!" Whip ordered.

"No! I'm sick of this bullshit, Whip! I'm done! I'm fucking done! I quit!" I screamed at the top of my lungs.

I stormed off, knowing Whip nor the club could afford another strike, or the city would snatch the license faster than you could say *gotcha, bitch.* The cops always made their way down to Bliss at closing, especially on the weekends. Not to mention the shooting that happened the night I met Kas. Every night, niggas left Bliss drunk, high, and sexually frustrated. It was no wonder they were always punching or shooting up something. Once I grabbed my shit from the locker room, I slid an unopened bottle of Ace of Spades from the supply closet into my duffel bag and kissed that hellhole goodbye once and for all.

After fifteen minutes of sitting in the car, giving Yara an angry play-by-play about what went down, the budding apprehension about managing my bills started to settle in. If I didn't go to work, I didn't get paid. I couldn't call PECO and explain that my run-in with a douchebag was the reason they wouldn't be getting their money on time. Frustrated, I slammed my fist against the steering wheel. I hadn't foreseen the night ending in chaos like that or me without a steady paycheck.

"Fuck! What the fuck did I just do?"

Fourteen

CANAAN

I LEFT the strip club with a chip on my shoulder, so it only felt right to blow off some steam. There was no way I was driving out to Connecticut to lay up with Trinity. So, I whipped out my phone to call up Yara to slide through. I knew all that shit she was talking about the last time being the last time was bullshit. If anything, I'd been sliding between those cheeks even more since her nigga put that ring on her finger.

An hour later, I had her lil booty bent over my bed, spread eagle with her hairless pussy in the air. I fucked her every which way, twisting her body like a rag doll. Yara gripped me tightly, nails clawing at my spine as she rode me. Her perky DD breast spilled against my bare chest as our tongues danced.

She broke the kiss and let her sweet, warm breath linger against my ear. "Oh fuck, yes! Yes! Right there! Don't stop! Don't you fuckin' stop!" She whimpered.

The hairs on the back of my neck prickled. She sounded so fuckin' good when she moaned like that. Yara gripped onto my thick muscular shoulders as I drew my tongue into her mouth. I reached around, slid a finger inside her tight ass, and continued to let her ride me until my seed spilled out. An exhausted sigh escaped my lips as my tired body crashed beside hers, heart kicking against my chest.

"You were going for the gold tonight, huh?" Yara asked before tangling her sepia brown body in my sheets.

"Yeah, well. I had to blow off some steam."

She reached up to tame her long, wild hair, pulling it into a high bun on top of her head. "Somethin' happen?"

"Got into it with some bitch in the club earlier tonight."

"What club?" she inquired.

"Bliss."

"Bliss? My homegirl works there. Well, *did,* I guess."

"What's her name?"

She cut her eyes at me. "Why? So you can go and harass her? The only female's name you need on that tongue is mine."

I rolled my eyes at her before lighting a blunt. "Yeah, yeah. Whatever. Let you tell it, you done with a nigga and shit."

"I thought I was, too," she answered while shrugging her slender, bare shoulders.

"Seems like you got some shit you need to figure out," I replied before passing her the blunt.

She puffed it twice before passing it back. "Guess I do."

I eyed her while I inhaled. With a slim build, big titties, and a pretty face, Yara was my type. She was beautiful, and I enjoyed her company when we were naked, but we both knew what it was. She had her situation, and I had mine. When we met, I thought she would be the type of jawn I hit and quit, but once I found out just how much power that lil pussy came with, we agreed to keep seeing each other casually. I didn't need to know her hopes and dreams or if she'd made time to eat every day. She had a full-time nigga for that shit. For that reason, I told her my last name was Mitchell. She didn't need to know what I did for a living or who my family was.

"I think you ruined me sexually. I've never had dick this good," she made known as we continued to get high together.

"Am I supposed to feel guilty about that? Because I don't."

Yara snickered. "You're an asshole. You know that?"

"My sister calls me that all the time."

"I didn't know you had a sister."

"You don't know a lot of things about me."

"Then tell me something," she insisted.

"Like what?"

"Anything about you."

"Since when do we do this?" I asked with a questioning brow.

"What?"

"Talk after we fuck."

She giggled. "I know, right."

"Is that what you want? For a nigga to talk ya fuckin' head off after I dick you down?" I asked, huffing out a chuckle.

She laughed a little harder. "Please don't. And I don't know. Maybe I'm starting to realize that change isn't always bad."

"Sounds like you talkin' about more than just us."

She sighed before passing the blunt from her fingers to mine. "We both know we can't keep doin' this."

"All you gotta do is say the word," I said with a shrug.

"And then that's it? That's the end?"

"What? You wanted me to chase you or somethin'?"

She sat up on her elbows. "I didn't say that. Everything is temporary. This is simply one of those things."

"Yeah, sure."

"What do you mean by that?" she asked in a tone that let me know she was trying to pick a fight.

I shook my head in a swift arc. "Nothin'."

"No, say it."

"Why? So you can look at me like I'm the bad guy for keepin' it a stack with you? I'm good."

Yara's head wagged from side to side. "No, I won't."

"Yeah, okay," I sneered.

"Just say it, Canaan, damn."

"Fine. You only want that fairytale shit because that's what you've been programmed to want, Yara. People like you and me are meant to be free. You don't have to only be with one person for the rest of your life, but that's the path you chose because society has hardwired women to chase after this idea of a happily ever after."

Yara crossed her arms beneath her juicy breasts. "My relationship isn't up for discussion," she snapped, declining to acknowledge what I'd said to her.

"Tell me you *don't* feel trapped, and I'll drop it," I promised her.

The room grew quiet. It was the first conversation we'd had that went past the surface level, and by how silent the room was, I knew it would likely be our last.

"I'm just trying to do the right thing. Why can't you see that?"

"I do. But if you really knew shit, you'd know that marriage ain't for everybody, and they damn sure ain't always about love. What we got goin' on is cool, but if you want to hop off the ride, I'm not going to stop you. The same door you used to get inside this mothafucka is the same one you can use to leave," I informed her before blowing my smoke out.

And with those words, she gathered her shit and left the room. Minutes later, I heard the front door slam behind her, and suddenly, we were back to being strangers.

Fifteen

JRUE

KAS'S CHECK cleared three days later, and *Jrue's Interiors* was *officially* back in business. I couldn't have met him at a better time, especially since I was no longer working at Bliss. He'd been my financial lifeline without even knowing it. As much as I hated the job, it was the highest-paying one I had, and it kept my head above water. Between gentrification and inflation, the square footage wasn't getting any more extensive, and the rent wasn't getting any cheaper. I lay on the couch, staring at the gold champagne bottle on the kitchen counter.

"So, are you gonna be the one to pop this shit open, or should I?" Yara asked from the kitchen.

"Guess I should, huh?"

"Um, duh. We should be celebrating your first huge client, J! I'll grab the glasses."

After I popped open the bottle, Yara filled our glasses. Bubbles foamed over the brim as I sloshed the expensive champagne around in my mouth. The texture was crisp and creamy. "Mmm. Tastes like luxury!"

"Wait! We were supposed to toast first, dummy!" she whined, screwing up the freckles on her nose and round cheeks.

I swiped my hand across my lips. "My bad! I'm ready. What are we toasting to?"

"To your success, Miss Entrepreneur of the year!"

"I don't know about all that, but thanks, girl. Cheers!"

"Cheers!"

Yara's expression lifted in a smile, causing the skin around her cocoa-brown eyes to crinkle. We'd been girls since our sophomore year at Cheyney University, the oldest HBCU in the country, where we were both communications majors. She had tawny brown skin, a slender frame, a set of perky DD breasts, and no ass. I was the opposite. I had ass and curves for days, and what seemed like bee stings for tits compared to hers.

"So, tell me about this new client of yours," she stated before sipping her champagne.

I shrugged lazily. "What's there to tell?"

"I don't know. What's he like?"

"To be honest, he's a hard ass, but…"

"But what?"

"Never mind. It's nothing."

She arched a questioning brow. "It's clearly something, and now I'm curious."

"Ugh," I grumbled, "he's so *damn* sexy."

Her arched brows heightened. "Uh oh."

"What?"

"Isn't he technically considered your boss?"

"So?"

"So? That should be a red flag for you. I'm concerned as to why it's not."

I sucked my teeth before pushing out a loud huff. "It's weird. I don't see him often, but it's always so… intense when I do. Electric, even. There's this unspoken chemistry between us. We don't have to say shit. We just… I don't know. We feel it," I confessed.

"Sounds like a WorkBae crush if I've ever heard of one."

My lean shoulders rose and fell in a lazy shrug as I sighed. "I don't know what it is."

"You know what they say about mixing business with pleasure," she said, trying to be the voice of reason.

"So that's what you would do? Steer clear of him because of business?"

"We ain't talkin' about me. We talkin' about you."

"And I'm asking your ass, what would you do, Yara? C'mon, tell me. I'm literally going crazy over here, thinking about this man way more than I should. Like, I shouldn't even have the time to think about him as much as I do with as busy as I am, but I do. And now you're telling me to stay away?"

Her hoop earrings shook from side to side. "I'm not saying anything. You're grown. And one thing about you, oh baby, Jrue gon' do what Jrue wanna do. You already know this, so I'm not wasting my damn breath."

I sighed. "Fine. Don't. And when I finish this project without bussin' it open for him, you'll owe me an *I told you so* drink."

She scoffed. "Yeah, right."

"You don't believe me, huh?"

"Only because I know your ass."

"What the hell is that supposed to mean?"

Yara shrugged her narrow shoulders. "You're too sexually... free and have way too much attraction to this man not to act on your impulses. It's only a matter of time before you're jumpin' WorkBae's bones."

I laughed. "Well, lucky for you, no one asked you."

Her arched brow creased. "You did, actually."

"Shut up! Enough about me. What about you? What's going on in your world?"

Yara shifted her weight on the couch before crushing a throw pillow against her chest. "As you know, it's wedding season, so work has been a fucking madhouse. I haven't even had a second to think about ideas for my own."

"Any new clients?"

"Girl, too many. Blake's old ass hasn't been laid since the Reagan Administration, so she makes sure to bide her time with other people's happily ever afters. I don't have a free weekend for the next two months!"

I chuckled. "Yikes. All work and no play make for a dry kitty."

Yara's laugh joined in with mine. "I know that's right."

"Keep it up, and you gon' be just like her," I warned.

She rolled her eyes skyward. "Please, don't wish that on me! I may be busy now, but I'm never too busy to sit on the right dick. Don't get it twisted."

"You can't say things like that. You're an engaged woman now!"

"Oh yeah! I forgot." She giggled while glancing at the diamond wrapped around her finger.

I cackled. "Yeah, yeah. But I'm the sexually free one, though, right?"

Yara rolled her cocoa-brown eyes. "Anyway, I sat in with Blake on a new consult a few days ago, and baby, the budget for this bride's wedding is bananas!" she dished. "I'm talking the dream wedding of all dream weddings. When I saw that five-hundred-thousand-dollar budget, I swear I gagged."

"Jesus! No one should be allowed to spend that much money on a wedding."

"I know, right."

"What about the bride? Does she seem like she's gonna be chill or a complete bridezilla?"

"Mmm. Too soon to tell. I can say that she's full of ideas. I think she was working with another planner at first, but something happened, and now she's working with us. Blake didn't give me the full details about her, but she *was* vague about her fiancé."

"What do you mean?"

"Well, Blake always has new couples fill out an intake questionnaire so we can get a feel for what stage of planning they're in, the couple's likes and dislikes, colors, etcetera. Everything for the groom's section was practically blank. She didn't even put his name."

I frowned. "What?"

"I don't know. It kinda almost seems like she's in an arranged marriage. Or like in some sort of *90-Day Fiancé* situation."

"Maybe she's marrying a prince from another country or a rich diplomat or something."

"Blake says she doesn't care what kind of marriage it is, as long as the check clears. She says our only job is to provide our brides a happy ever after. What happens after their magical day is on them."

"I can't blame her. Make that money, honey."

Yara giggled. "Don't let it make you."

Three weeks later

KAS SAT across the conference table from me as we listened to the presenter go over safety code training. It was the first time I'd seen him in weeks, except for a few quick head nods in passing. We'd both been busy, but somehow fate had tossed us back into each other's presence. My phone buzzed in my lap with a text from Yara, stealing my attention from the presenter.

Yara: *Are we still on for drinks at six at Louie's?*

Me: *Yup. I can't wait.*

I'd been hard at work, choosing paint colors and finishes, pieces of furniture, rugs, and even art from local black artists that we hadn't had time to catch up and dish on life in a while. When I was coming, she was going. I remained lost in thought, eyes trained on the presenter's lips as he talked, but retaining nothing. I glanced down at my phone, expecting to see another text from Yara. Instead, Kas's name was across my screen. I nervously clicked it.

Kas: *Pay attention. Jk.*

I glanced up at him, realizing his eyes were already zeroed in on me. He smirked. I dropped my eyes back down to my phone to text my reply.

Me: *I'm sorry, but this is boring.*

Kas: *It is. You wanna ditch for a bit?*

Me: *Isn't that breaking the rules?*

Kas: *I'm technically your boss, and if I say it's cool, then it's cool.*

TEN MINUTES LATER, we took a break for lunch. After stepping away from the table, I found Kas standing outside the door, waiting for me.

My lips twisted. "Let me guess. You knew there was a break coming up."

He smirked. "I might've had a clue, but freedom is freedom, right? So, you welcome."

"I guess I should thank you. With all that staring you were doing, it was getting hard for me to pay attention," I joked.

"My bad. I was distracting you?"

"Absolutely."

"What would you rather I put my eyes on?" he quizzed while arching a questioning brow.

My face flushed with lust. I dared not look up and lock eyes with him. He would've known I was completely under his spell if I had. Yara was wrong. It was more than a girlish crush.

"You wanna see what I've been working on lately in the condo upstairs?" I asked, quickly switching gears.

"Sure."

I walked ahead of him, trying to put a little distance between us before we were trapped inside a metal box together. My finger jabbed the silver button, and in seconds, the elevator lifted us skyward. The ride was so smooth it barely felt like we were moving at all. I stole a glance at his reflection in the clean metal doors, no smudges or fingerprints in sight, before pinging my eyes to the built-in speaker above us and then watching the floor numbers change. We'd almost made it to the twentieth floor without so much as an awkward stomach growl when he spoke up. "By the way, I like your hair like that," he stated, complimenting my high bun with a few loose spiral curls at the nape of my neck and sideburns.

I clutched the metal handrail before swiping a curl behind my ear. My racing heartbeat stabbed at my eardrums. "Oh, um, thanks."

"You should wear it like that more often."

The elevator chimed, and the metal doors began to open before he could force a response from me. I couldn't have been more grateful for the opportunity to put some distance between us. The minute we stepped inside the condo, the ambiance was chill.

"It's nowhere near finished, but it's coming along," I expressed while walking up to the second level of the loft-style condo and looking over the railing at him.

There was a couch set with mixed textures of leather and velvet stationed in the living room, with a large round coffee table right in the center of the floor to bring it all together. I wanted it so that no matter where someone chose to sit in the living room, they'd always have the best seat in the house. There was still quite a lot of floor space to cover, and I knew an oversized Persian rug would do the trick.

I made my way back down to him. The entire room was swallowed up by sunlight, but when you wanted privacy, all you had to do was click the automatic floor-to-ceiling blackout curtains. The whole place was innovative, from the security system to everyday household needs like the thermostat, heated bathroom floors, and video doorbell.

"It's looking good."

I glanced at him, and a smile crawled up my face. "Thanks."

Each time I stole a glance at him, I noticed something different. This time it was the vacant holes in his ears and the scar across the knuckles on his left hand. Before that, it was the breadth of his shoulders. Before that, the tattoo on his neck. The longer I allowed my eyes to linger, the louder Yara's voice got in the back of my head, telling me *not* to mix business with pleasure. If I didn't run while I had the chance, I would've surely melted underneath his gaze.

"Well, I'm gonna go grab a bite to eat before our lunch break is up. I'll, uh, see you back in class?"

"Yup," he responded while dipping his chin in a quick nod.

A FEW HOURS LATER, I waited for the elevator to ding while fumbling with the strap and clasp on my left heel. I'd swapped them out for a pair of flats after the meeting ended and had been working nonstop ever since. I glanced down at my phone. It was already fifteen minutes to six. There was no way I was making it to the bar to meet Yara on time. I was already flustered enough with my shoe, and waiting over five minutes for an elevator in a practically empty building was making matters worse.

"Oh, come on," I griped, aggressively jabbing the elevator button a few times.

After another unsuccessful attempt at securing the strap around my exposed ankle, I got so mad I tossed my heel just as the shiny doors parted. To my surprise, Kas was standing on the other side with a confused look and my heel in his hand.

My eyes widened. "Oh my God! I'm so sorry!" I winced. "Did I hit you with my shoe?"

"I've got quick hands. I caught it. You look like you've got somewhere to be," he stated, passing it back to me.

I dipped my chin. "Yeah. I'm kind of in a rush. Late for drinks with my best friend."

"Drinks? Sounds fun."

I leaned to the side, still unable to fasten the clasp by the time the elevator reached the bottom floor. "Yeah," I answered, distractedly.

The doors opened, and Kas leaned down, shifting his hands from his sides to my calf to steady my balance. "Hold still and relax. I got you."

My breath hitched before I etched out a slow, steady exhale. His palms skimmed across my satin smooth calf muscle, giving it a slight squeeze to keep me steady. I gripped the railing for extra balance as his hands coasted down to my ankle before he fastened my shoe and then the other.

"T-thanks," I stammered while easing my foot from his grasp as he stood.

"Have a good night, Jrue."

The elevator door closed, and I couldn't stop replaying our intimate moment over and over in my head. Just when I thought it was safe to breathe, he'd gone and snatched my heart right out of my chest.

Sixteen

KAS

RAINDROPS PATTERED against my arms as I marched inside the art gallery where Cena worked. Upon entering, I noticed only a few large pieces on the plain white walls leading to the reception desk. The gallery used to be an abandoned warehouse and had since been purchased and rehabbed by her family, who turned it into one of the most prestigious galleries in Philly. I shuffled across the shiny wood floors, searching the ample, open space for Cena until I spotted her discussing a piece with a potential buyer.

I kept myself occupied by examining the framed paintings and sculptures while she wrapped up.

"Hey, you," she called out, heels clicking and clacking as she inched closer to me. Black denim covered her hips, and a gray sweater hung off the edges of her shoulders while she stood tall on a pair of knee-high stiletto boots.

We shared a quick embrace before separating. "What's up? Is now still a good time for lunch?" I asked.

She shook her head. "About that. I've got a private showing in the next hour that I can't miss. Can I, um, get a rain check?"

I bobbed my head. "Sure. No problem."

"I'm sorry. I know we have things to talk about, y'know, for the wedding."

"Yeah."

"The wedding planners keep texting me about the flowers. What do you think about red roses instead of white for the ceremony? They say red is more *romantic*," she said with an eye roll and a slight giggle.

I shook my head before replying. "Whatever you want for that jawn is fine."

The more the weeks started to fly by, the closer the wedding date seemed to be approaching. Cena was a cool, ambitious, and beautiful woman, but I still couldn't erase Jrue from my mind. I'd seen her every day for the past six weeks, only if it was for a split second. As time edged on, it became harder for me to fight my attraction to her, but I still hadn't made a move because of my commitment and my unwillingness to disappoint Cena's family and my own.

"Well, they have the venue, caterers, DJ, live band, photographer, and uh, damn, oh, the videographer, too. All that's booked."

"Seems like you've been working. I'm sure it'll be dope."

"Oh! Before I go, do you have any input on where you'd wanna go after? Y'know, for the... honeymoon?" she quizzed while shifting her weight from one heel to the other.

My eyes bugged a little at the mere mention of honeymoon. I was so hung up on not wanting to be married that I hadn't stopped to think about what all came after the wedding.

"Wow, uh. That's, uh, a lot to digest."

"Tell me about it."

"I'll put some thought into it and, uh, let you know," I stated while pulling my vibrating phone from my pocket. "Hey, I gotta take this. I'll let you get back to your day."

"Yeah, sure. Thanks for coming by, Kas," she said with a smile.

I dipped my chin. "No problem," I replied before clicking accept to answer my father's call. "Yeah?"

"Where are you?"

"Leavin' the McQueen's art gallery in Midtown Village. We were supposed to have lunch and talk over some wedding stuff, but she got caught up at work," I explained.

"Finally coming around to the idea, huh?"

I swung my head in a no. "Not exactly."

"I don't know why you insist on fighting it. It's not like Cena's a dog. She's a beautiful young woman."

"It ain't about her looks."

"What's it about then?"

I made sure I was inside the privacy of my car before providing my answer. "Kamil told me you've been sending Silas McQueen money for years. What's that about, and why didn't you tell me?" I confronted him.

He sighed, knowing he had no choice but to provide me an answer. "They were loans."

"Loans? What kind of loans?"

"He's got a gambling problem. Has had the addiction for years, but it kicked up even more after his wife died."

"What's that got to do with you?"

"With a gambling addiction comes gambling debt. He's in the hole for millions, Kas."

"With you?"

"Not just our family."

"You've been loaning him money to pay off his gambling debts for years and he still won't give you the territory you want to expand?" I quizzed.

"Silas McQueen owes me more than you know."

"If that's the truth, then why do you still have to prove your loyalty and strengthen a bond you already say is strong? There's something you're not telling me. What aren't you telling me, Pa?" I pressed him. "If I'm going to go through with this for you, I need to know the whole truth. Right now!" I demanded.

"When McQueen came to me about the money, I knew he needed more than just that. With his gambling debts, loss of his wife, and his failing health, he knew he looked weak as a boss and needed strength to bring up his family. So, he suggested the merger between our families."

"And in return, you got the territory?"

"More than I initially asked for, yes. Besides, I told you and your brother about my deal with the Simms family."

"That still stands? How? Why after what they did?"

"I want Silas and his entire family out."

My brow creased. "W-what do you mean out?"

"Out of *The Order* for good."

"What? Why? I thought you said that Silas—w-why make an alliance with a family you want to try and push out?"

"What do you want me to do? Kill the man's entire family and take his territory? No. That would cause an all-out mutiny within *The Order*, but he's gotten sloppy, Kasim. Shipments are missing. His payments to me are late or half paid. And I'm not the only one he's doing business with who has noticed."

"What was the exact deal you made with Douglass Simms, Pa?"

"It's what I told you it was, but my long-term plan is to oust the entire McQueen family altogether."

"W-why? I don't understand."

"Once the Montgomery soldiers come in and start dealing so close to the McQueens, they will have their own turf war. We know Silas is weak, but, if necessary, I will aid Douglass in wiping out the McQueen family so they can take their place in *The Order*."

My ears were burning by the time my father stopped talking. "Kamil was right, Pa. Are you trying to start a war?"

"If it comes to it, then yes. Douglass is willing to play by my rules and build his way up to securing his place in *The Order*, but his son, Desmond, he's thirsty for it now. I can tell by how he moves. I've got my eye on them both. But don't worry; everything will work out in our favor in the end."

My head wagged from left to right in disbelief. My father sounded like a traitor, but he kept insisting everything was fine and under control. That only meant he didn't have a handle on shit the way he thought he did.

"I still don't want to do this," I confessed, grumbling as I spoke.

He sighed into the receiver. "What's disappointing is your unwillingness to put your own shit aside for your family. It speaks volumes, Kasim!"

My forehead creased as rage burned through my body. "I'm not unwilling. I'm just trying to be resourceful and think of another way that doesn't involve me marryin' somebody I barely know!"

"I've let you go this long, leaving you to do whatever it was that you wanted to do. And now, when I call on you, all I've heard since is questions and backtalk! If you weren't my son, I would've had my soldiers slice off your tongue!" He snarled. "If I didn't know better, I'd say someone already has your attention."

I paused. "What if they do?"

"Is she from a family within *The Order*?"

"No."

"Does she come from money?"

"Why does that matter?"

"You can't bring anyone into our fold. Everyone isn't equipped to adapt to our lifestyle. How many fucking times do I have to tell you that?" He sighed before continuing. "Look, you're a smart, handsome young man, Kasim. And I understand your hesitancy to tie yourself down to one woman. It's natural."

"What are you saying?" I asked, thinking I may have broken through to him.

"I'm saying all this to say, do whatever you want on the side, but your wedding to Cena McQueen *will* happen, Kasim. And that's an order," he decreed, pulling rank before ending the call.

I'D BEEN in a shitty mood ever since the call with my father. Everything changed the minute I stormed into the building lobby. My eyes gravitated straight to Jrue, who was standing barefoot on a two-story extension ladder with a paintbrush in her hands. I couldn't help but notice her physique from behind. She had a set of slim legs that I could see wrapped around my waist and an ass I wouldn't mind pulling up behind. My dick hardened to stone in my slacks at the thought. Her heels laid against the tarp spread out underneath the ladder as she reached up, extending her arm to the ceiling. The ladder wobbled, and my heart thudded in my chest as I rushed over to stabilize it.

I called out to her with concern laced in my voice. "Yo, be careful. What the hell are you doin' up there anyway?"

She snapped her neck down and then focused her attention on the wall. "This isn't my first time on a ladder, Kas. I'm okay."

"What are you doing up there?"

"If you want something done right, sometimes you have to do it yourself," she replied.

I watched her reach up, extending her arm again, but still unable to reach the spot she was trying to get, making me chuckle. "You're a bit of a control freak, huh?"

She lowered her arm before turning to face me. "I prefer perfectionist," she stated while batting her lengthy, black lashes.

I laughed again. "I bet you would. Here, get down and let me help," I offered.

Jrue rolled her brown eyes to the ceiling before inching down the ladder. "I'm only giving this to you because you're taller than me," she stated before extending the brush to me.

I slid off my blazer just as my cell vibrated in my pocket. I pulled it out to see my father's name across the screen before pressing ignore. I took Jrue's place on the ladder, painting the spot she'd been trying to get.

"How's it lookin' from down there?" I asked her.

"Looks good. *Real good*," she replied.

I slowly retracted the ladder before placing the brush in the drip pan. A compelling feeling of curiosity washed over me as I stepped to her. "What's really good with you?" I asked.

"What do you mean?"

"What's your story? I mean, I remember some shit from the club when we first met, but..."

"But what?"

"I can't lie. You got me a lil curious."

"About me?"

"Yeah."

"Why?"

I shot her a lazy shrug. "I wish I knew."

"What all do you remember from the club?" she inquired, licking her cupid's bow.

The way the tip of her tongue grazed the top of her lips instantly drew my attention to them. "Damn…"

"What?"

My neck fluttered side to side, trying to stop my mind from derailing. "Nothin', um, let's see. You're a Philly jawn, born and bred. And you're… twenty-five?"

She nodded. "Yup, and yup. I'll be twenty-six on Halloween."

"You're a Scorpio?"

"Yeah. You got a problem with that?"

"The contrary. My birthday is two days after yours."

"Ayyyeee! Scorpio gang!" she cheered.

"The best to ever do it," I added.

Jrue swiped all of her hair from one side of her neck to the other, allowing me a glimpse of her suckable neck and collarbone. "So, that's all you remember from the club?"

"You willing to tell me more?"

"That depends."

"On?" I asked, inching closer.

"What it is you wanna know."

"You think we could continue this conversation over dinner? I like talkin' to you."

"I like talking to you, too. As far as dinner goes, were you thinking tonight or—"

"Yeah."

Her face went from cheerful to unreadable in the blink of an eye. "It's not that I don't want to; it's just—"

"What?"

"It's just… you're my first, *big* client, and I wanna be professional."

"Then be professional."

"I can't when you… never mind." She paused while wagging her head.

"Nah, tell me."

She flashed her lustful eyes up at me. "When you're looking at me the way you're looking at me."

"How am I looking at you, Jrue?"

"Like you wanna take me down right here, right now."

I stepped back while resting my hand on my beard. She wasn't wrong, but I respected that she was putting her money first. "I apologize if I've made you uncomfortable."

She shook her head. "It's the opposite of uncomfortable, Kas. But thanks for the invite and the chat."

I tipped my head forward while picking up my blazer. "Anytime."

On my way to the elevator, my phone vibrated again. This time, Kamil was calling. "Yeah?" I answered, stepping inside to press the penthouse button.

"Pa said he's been callin' you, and you not answerin'. What's up?"

"Mind your business, ak."

"I would if I could, but we got *The Order* business to handle. I'm on my way to the building now. You there?"

"Yeah. I was just about to head up to the penthouse."

"Good. We got the niggas who were in the car the night Koda was killed. I left the one who pulled the trigger for you to deal with. I figured you'd want to question him first."

"Bring that mothafucka straight to me."

"I'll have the guys deliver the package to you in thirty."

"Have 'em take the service elevator, Mil. And be discreet. I got workers here," I warned him.

THE ELEVATOR DOORS PARTED, opening to the penthouse. I stepped across the tarp, unbuttoning my cuff and pushing my sleeves up my forearm. The entire space was equipped with the latest technology, including high-tech security cameras from the Underwoods. There was a room dedicated to only weapons, which was our family's specialty. Machine guns, Uzis, Desert Eagles, and AK-47s all decorated the walls, begging me to select them as my weapon of choice. Soon, I heard the rumbling noise of Kamil and my father's men entering the space, notifying me that my package had been delivered. I stepped out to see a man with his wrists bound above his head and mouth gagged. My father's men parted like the Red Sea as I marched toward him. Gun drawn, adrenaline pumped through my veins. In the weeks since Koda's death, we'd managed to find his safe houses and stash houses, but not him. And I knew things wouldn't officially be over until whoever ordered the hit, was dead.

"Who ordered the hit outside of the club? Was it Douglass Simms?" I asked, wasting no time aiming my handgun at his throat. My finger grazed the trigger.

I removed the drool-soaked bandanna from his mouth, allowing him to answer. "I—I don't know," he stammered in a panic.

Beads of sweat coated his hairline as I wagged my head back and forth. "Wrong answer. I don't think you fully understand the situation you're in. You thought you could fuck with our family, and we wouldn't fuck with you back?"

"I—I—"

His eyes widened as I watched the fear in his teary orbs turn to peace. He knew the life he'd signed up for. He was going to die and awaited death openly and without hesitation.

"Let me guess, you don't know?" I crashed my closed fist into his nose and immediately heard the bones snap.

He cried out in pain as his bright, red blood splattered against his skin. Unable to hold his nose or contain the bleeding, it continued to drip in thick trails down his lips and chin.

"P-please. I—I will tell you w-what I know."

A sinister grin spread across my lips. "Now that's more like it. Speak up and speak clear."

"I—I heard t-through the rumor mill that D-Desmond Simms made the call t-to move in on the McQueen's t-territory. Then when our men got killed, we got ordered to do the hit, t-that's all I know."

Darkness crossed my eyes as I glared at him without blinking. "Who ordered you to do the hit at the club that night? Was it Desmond Simms?"

"I don't know. I swear I don't know!" he shouted. "Please, just kill me!"

My palm cupped his throat, squeezing him as he wheezed for air. "What do you think, Kamil? You think he's lyin' to me?"

Kamil shook his head. "You don't wanna lie to him. Trust me."

I squeezed his throat tighter. "My brother's right, y'know? You don't wanna lie to me," I advised.

I released my grasp long enough for him to draw in his next breath and answer my question. "I swear to you. I'm not lying. I don't know!" he choked out before coughing.

Frustrated, I drew my arm back before slamming the butt of my gun across his face, instantly knocking him unconscious. "Take him out back," I ordered my father's soldiers. "I want this to be quick."

We reconvened outside, and Kamil joined me while I watched my soldiers drag the mark out by his limbs before tossing him into a deep hole near a cement mixer on site. We knew we didn't have to do the dirty work ourselves. We had soldiers to do that shit for us, but I wasn't going to be satisfied unless I was the one behind the trigger that killed the man who ordered the hit that killed Koda. Besides, over the years, a part of me had grown to enjoy the art of killing. I enjoyed the endorphin high that came from it.

The mark woke up the minute his body hit the cold, hard ground.

"I'm gonna ask you again. Did Desmond Simms order the hit at the club that night?" I asked before motioning for one of my men to turn on the mixer.

I couldn't hear shit over the loud whirring sound, so I studied his body language instead. I was looking for a head nod, but all he gave me were muted screams and wails as wet concrete plopped out, filling the hole little by little. I started into the hole, watching the cement harden around his limbs, weighing him down. He fought to get out, squirming and squiggling, but the harder he fought, the more it became like quicksand. Before the cement drowned him by covering his nostrils, I put two bullets in his forehead without mercy or a second thought.

"Consider this a message," I mumbled.

There was no mercy for enemies or those who went against *The Order*. In the end, we always got our revenge, one way or another. I didn't move until each shell was covered. After filling the hole, I waved my hand, signaling the mixer to be cut off. I tucked my gun in the back of my pants and headed back into the building. The familiar euphoric feeling that coursed through my veins, like hot cocoa on a cold winter day after taking a life, was missing. Nothing felt the same since Jrue had taken over as the center of attention in my mind.

Silence blanketed the space when I stepped back inside the penthouse to shower and clean his blood off me. I considered the fact that he probably didn't know anything. He'd been hired to do a job. He was expendable muscle. I wasn't sure he could've even picked out Douglass Simms in a lineup. But I didn't care if I had to leave a trail of bodies in my wake; I was going to avenge Koda's death if it was the last thing I did.

As much as I didn't want to speak to my father, I called to inform him of the news from the mark.

"Has the package been shipped?" he asked in code.

"Yes. We need to talk."

I couldn't risk telling him over the phone that I knew who'd ordered Douglass Simms' soldiers to move into the McQueen territory too early. Desmond Simms was his son and just as blood thirsty for his father's seat as Canaan was.

"Meet me at the house."

"I'm on the way."

JRUE

I'D JUST FINISHED STAGING the master bedroom and took a minute to sit across the bed with my feet propped up and enjoyed my private view of downtown Philly's beautiful morning skyline. It was probably my favorite room in the space because of the view. That, and because it had a closet to die for. My phone rang, snapping me out of my moment of peace. I swiped to answer Yara's FaceTime call and heard her frantic voice as soon as it connected.

"Oh my God!" she shrieked.

"What's wrong?"

"The ceiling is leaking! Everywhere!"

My brows heightened in shock. "What! What do you mean? What happened?"

"The fuckin' bathroom pipes in the apartment above us burst!"

"They what!"

"He came down about an hour ago saying his toilet flooded and that he was waiting on maintenance. He came back twenty minutes ago saying maintenance said a pipe burst, and sure enough, our ceiling starts fucking raining!" she griped.

I let out a frustrated sigh. "How bad is it?"

"Bad enough for me to call you! I was getting ready for work when all this shit started happening!"

"Okay, okay. What do you need me to do?"

She paused long enough to look into the camera and roll her eyes at me. "Come home, Jrue! Duh!"

I smacked my lips. "I meant besides that. Do you need me to grab anything from the store?"

"Yeah. Towels and buckets. Lots and lots of fuckin' buckets!" she answered before ending the call.

"So much for my peace," I mumbled before getting off the bed to grab my things.

I ran into Kas on my way out of the building. He stopped in his tracks when he saw me. "Jrue, I'm glad I caught you."

"Yeah?"

"I've been meaning to check in with you."

"About what?" I snapped, instantly regretting my tone.

"What's wrong?"

"What makes you think somethings wrong?"

"The look on your face is a dead giveaway."

My neck fish-tailed from left to right. "I'm sorry for snapping at you like that. My roommate just called and said the pipes in the apartment above ours burst, so our shit is leaking. I've gotta get home to help her."

"Take a breath and tell me what you need," he said, sending chills down my spine.

I followed his lead and drew a deep breath through my nose before pushing it through my mouth. "Apparently, lots of towels and buckets. But don't worry about it. We'll be fine. Did you need something from me?" I quizzed, changing the subject.

"You sure?"

I dipped my chin in a quick nod. "Yeah."

"Okay, well, I need you to put together a presentation on where you are with the project, along with a few key talking points for the press."

"When do you need it by?"

"I was going to say the weekend, but now that I know you've got some personal shit to deal with, I'll say as soon as you can."

"Yeah, okay. Thanks."

"I hope everything works out with your apartment. Keep me posted."

"Um, sure. Thanks."

When I got home, Yara had buckets, bowls, and glasses throughout the hallway and in our bedrooms. We spent the better half of our day taking photos of the damage and moving all of our shit into the living room since the leak had caused damage in both of our bedrooms. It didn't take long for maintenance and the leasing office to determine the damage was too extensive to have us continue to stay there. The only thing left to do was terminate our lease and find a new place to live.

Two weeks later

THE AROMA of freshly brewed coffee, sweet caramel, and fresh-baked muffins drifted past my nose as I stepped inside the coffee house a couple of blocks from Kas's building. The scent momentarily brushed away the stress of everything I'd been dealing with since our apartment flooded. The last thing Yara and I planned for was an unexpected move. Luckily, we were both financially willing and able to upgrade to a bigger space, and we negotiated a quick move-in date because of the circumstances. The only downside was that Yara was stuck working a wedding and wouldn't be around to help me pick up the U-Haul or move.

My teeth sunk into the warm blueberry muffin as I advanced up to the door and headed down the block.

"Jrue," I heard Kas call out from a few steps behind me.

I snapped my neck in his direction while licking crumbs from my lips. "Kas. Hey."

"I didn't know you liked coffee."

"Like it? My birthstone is a legit coffee bean," I joked before pressing my lips up to the side of the scalding coffee cup. After a quick sip, the warmth cascaded down my throat.

"How goes the apartment search?"

"It's good. We're, uh, moving into our new place this weekend."

His smile swooped to one side as we trekked over the crosswalk. "That's what's up."

I nodded hesitantly before shooting my eyes to the ground. "Yeah..."

"What's wrong?"

"Nothing. It's nothing. Uh, did you ever get a chance to look over what I sent you?" I quizzed, changing the subject.

While salvaging what furniture hadn't been damaged and packing, I managed to get Kas the presentation and talking points about the project within a few days. I'd been splitting my time between my personal woes and professional duties and hadn't laid eyes on him until then.

"To be honest with you, no. I haven't forgotten about that jawn. I just have to move some things around and make the time," he admitted while tilting his coffee cup to his pouty, brown lips.

"No rush. I just wanted to make sure I got you any feedback."

"Tell you what, let's do it Saturday."

"I'll be moving Saturday, remember."

"Damn. You did say that, didn't you?"

I let out a soft chuckle. "Yeah, I did."

He stepped ahead of me and opened the door. "Well, do you need help?"

My brows lifted. "Uh, yeah, actually. I do."

"Say less. Text me your address, and I'll have the truck there by eight."

He let the words roll off his tongue so effortlessly that I had to question if he was serious. "Wait. You're–you're serious?" I asked as we trudged inside the elevator, and I pressed the button to my floor.

Kas dipped his bearded chin. "Yeah. I'll see you Saturday morning."

The elevator dinged, and I didn't dare tell him no thanks or never mind. Instead, I nodded. I wouldn't mind the company or the extra manpower.

"Thanks... um, have a, um, good day," I told him.

I watched him press the button to the penthouse level before he glanced up at me. "You too."

SATURDAY MORNING ROLLED AROUND, and I heard a loud honk outside my living room window. I glanced out of the blinds, and my eyes widened. A large moving truck was parked across the street, and four men were making their way to my building. Minutes later, there was a knock on my door. I opened it to see Kas standing there. The first thing I noticed was his fresh haircut. The next was the white tee and camouflage pants he was wearing. Both his ears and left wrist were shining, and he held two cups of coffee in his hands.

"Good morning."

"Good morning."

"You all packed and ready? I got the movers here."

I smirked, allowing him and the movers he'd hired to step inside. "Yeah. When you said truck, I thought you meant a U-Haul."

"Nah. I figured we could review your talking points and the presentation while the guys get to work. Kill two jawns with one stone, ya know?"

I bobbed my chin. "Uh, yeah. Sure."

"You good?"

"Yeah. I'm just a little shocked my client is helping me move everything I have to my name," I admitted.

Kas cocked his head to the side. "Is that all you see me as?"

"N–no," I stammered, "I didn't mean to offend you. I only meant that–"

The muscles in his face relaxed as he belted out a quick laugh. "Relax, I'm kidding."

"So, was there anything you wanted me to discuss in the presentation or the talking points? Or was there something you didn't understand?"

"I understood it perfectly. I just like hearing you talk," he admitted with a smile.

The corners of my mouth lifted. "Kas..."

"What made you want to get into decorating and shit?"

I shrugged nervously. "I don't know. I—"

"Of course you do."

"What makes you think that?"

"Because it's your career, ain't it?"

"I'm the one who should be asking you about business. You're the one with the real estate game on lock with these buildings and restaurants. You don't just stumble into that. Interior design was exactly that for me. It was a hobby that stumbled into a business."

"So, you didn't go to school for it or anything?"

"No. I graduated from Cheyney University with a bachelor's degree in communications. I wanted to be a newscaster. And somehow, life happened, and amongst all my other jobs, decorating had always been a hobby of mine, y'know, but I never saw it as something lucrative. So, all this entrepreneurship stuff is still fresh to me," I admitted.

"How'd you end up working at Bliss?"

I shrugged. "You mean besides the fact that I needed a job with good tips?"

"True."

"Wanna know the craziest thing about that entire experience?"

"What?"

"The first time I stepped foot inside a strip club was when I went in for my interview."

"Really?"

"Yeah. I didn't know what I was getting into, but I knew I needed money, so yeah."

"You still workin' there?"

"Nah. I quit in a crazy blaze of glory a little after we started working together."

He chuckled. "Oh, I gotta hear that story."

"Not much to tell. I was in VIP. A nigga got handsy, so I got handsy back, just not in a nice way. Then he started lettin' the word bitch fall out his mouth all reckless and shit. Security had to hold me back. It was a mess."

His expression was stern, cold even. "Hold up. Somebody touched you?"

"Yeah, but it's okay. Don't worry, I got my lick back."

I could tell he was still tense about it, so I reached out to place my hand on his chest for reassurance. His heart was beating so hard I thought it would burst through his skin. "A—are you okay?"

"Did you get a name?"

"What? No. I mean, maybe, but I don't even remember it at this point. It's no big deal."

"It is. You should've had someone there protecting you."

"I'm a big girl, Kas. I can handle myself. Besides, that's what security was for. They swooped in and everything was fine."

He pressed his lips together in a hard line, while trying to calm himself down. Visibly, I could still tell he was uncomfortable. "I'm glad you're not working there anymore."

"Yeah. That makes two of us."

FOUR HOURS LATER, Kas and I plopped down on the couch in the new place. The movers had placed all the boxes and totes in the appropriate rooms and put our furniture together.

"That was by far the easiest move of my life. Thank you so much for all your help," I told him.

"I barely lifted a finger."

I shrugged. "Yeah, well, help is help. Are you hungry?"

"Why? You cookin'?"

"Um, no. Not one pot nor pan will be getting unpacked right this second. I was thinking about ordering in for lunch. Y'know, like Thai or something."

"Thai is cool," he agreed.

"Alright, then. Thai it is. Do you know what you want?"

"Shrimp fried rice is cool with me."

I smirked. "Don't be tryna be like me."

"Whatever. I bet you don't eat that jawn how I do."

I clenched my thighs. "How do you eat it, Kas?"

"I put sweet Chile sauce on top. It's amazing," he said while imitating a chef's kiss.

"Oh, you ain't gotta tell me. That's the *only* way I eat it."

"That's what's up."

I placed an order with the nearest Thai restaurant and shot Yara a quick text to let her know everything with our move had been completed, so she could focus entirely on the wedding she was executing from start to finish.

Me: *Good luck today! BTW, the move is complete!!!*

Yara: *Thanks. And what do you mean complete? Did you leave half our shit on the street, Jrue?!*

Me: *LOL, no! I'll send you a pic in a minute, but complete, like, all our shit is in the new place.*

Yara: *How in the hell did you swing that? I thought for sure you'd be moving boxes until midnight.*

Me: *Let's just say I had a little help.*

Yara: *From WorkBae? You know what, don't answer that.*

Me: *He's still here. We're about to have lunch.*

Yara: *Bye, friend. Tell WorkBae thanks.*

Me: *I will.*

"My roommate says thank you," I told him as I walked over to one of the boxes stacked in the corner and ripped it open. After digging inside, I pulled out my Bluetooth speaker and plugged it in.

"You're both more than welcome."

After connecting my phone to the speaker, I put on a lo-fi hip-hop playlist for some background noise. Without our TV and internet set up, our voices easily echoed through the space. "I've got an idea."

"What?"

I sat back on the couch. "Let's play a game while we wait for the food to get here."

"What did you have in mind?"

"Earlier this week, you said you were curious about me."

"So?"

"So, I think it's only fair that I know things about you too. So, I'm going to ask you questions, and you've gotta answer them."

"Do I get to ask any questions in return?"

"Nope. Not this time. I'm putting you in the hot seat."

"What do you wanna know?"

"Wait! Before I start, is there anything off-limits that I *can't* ask about?"

"Nah. Go ahead."

"Okay, fine. What's upstairs in the penthouse?"

"You want me to show you?"

My brows creased. "Seriously?"

"No."

I smirked while folding my arms across my chest. "Mmm. The secrecy continues, huh?"

"Yeah."

"Fine. What initially made you interested in giving my business a chance?"

"Your passion and drive."

"Tell me the story of your first love."

"It's still being written," he answered, eyes boring into mine.

"Mmm. You've got an answer for everything, huh?"

"You haven't asked me anything hard yet," he stated.

Kas still hadn't bothered to tear his eyes away from mine. I twisted my lips to the side while changing my position on the couch. "You're doing it again," I reminded him.

"What?"

"Looking at me the way you do."

He arched one brow and angled his head to the side. "Do you want me to stop?"

"Is it wrong if I say no?"

"Not if it's what you want."

I sighed. "I told you, I wanna be professional."

"That's your favorite word, huh?" he joked, "but we're not at the job site right now."

I swallowed hard as my heart rate escalated. "Kas, I know, but—" Before the words could finish escaping my lips, there was a knock on the door. "I–I should get that."

He leaned in and placed his hand on my thigh. "It can wait."

"Kas–" I breathed.

He drew his face closer to mine. "Tell me to stop, and I'll stop."

I toyed with the thought in my mind for a tenth of a second before pressing my lips against his, letting Kas know my feigning disinterest was all cap. His lips were warm, moist, and inviting as hell. My hips thrust forward, propelling me into his lap as he placed his hands on the back of my neck, pulling me in to enjoy a deeper kiss. Our bodies melted together, limbs intertwining like branches on a tree until another knock sounded on the door. I slowly peeled myself away from him. "I'll be right back."

NO MATTER how hard I tried, I couldn't pry my thoughts away from Kas. Luckily, when I got up to answer the door and get the food, he got an emergency call and had to leave. Lord knows, if it hadn't been for that, he would've had my toes pointed to the ceiling in no time. After taking a shower and putting my new showerhead to good use, I turned on some music and started unpacking my things, hoping it would get my head out of the gutter.

Two hours later, I was heading to my mom's house to get my original birth certificate. When our apartment flooded, my passport got damaged, so I needed to start the process of getting a new one. When I arrived, I saw my sister Charity star fished across the couch as soon as I walked through the door.

"Is Mom here?" I asked her.

"No. She's working at the hospital. Why?"

"I knew I should've called on my way here."

"What's wrong?"

"Nothing. I need my birth certificate. Does she still keep all our important stuff locked upstairs in her closet safe?"

Charity shrugged. "I don't know. Maybe."

"You're no damn help."

"I'm seventeen. Why do I care where my birth certificate is?"

I rolled my eyes before hitting the steps. After searching the back of her closet for her safe and coming up with nothing, I made my way back downstairs. "You find it?" Charity asked from the kitchen.

I walked over to her while shaking my head. "Nope."

"Want a pizza roll?" she offered, pulling a baking tray full of them from the oven.

I wagged my head. "No."

She turned her attention to the TV in the living room. "We should do that."

"Do what?"

"That," Charity said, pointing at the screen.

I turned my attention to the Twenty-Three and Me commercial that was playing. "You wanna do a DNA test?"

"Yeah. Why not?"

"Since when are you interested in ancestry?"

"Mom is on my ass about applying for scholarships. If we do it, maybe I'll find out I'm like seventeen percent Filipino, and I can apply for even more minority scholarships."

I held the laugh on the tip of my tongue. "You're an idiot."

"Or am I?" she asked, tapping the side of her head. "Smells like effort to me, but what do I know?"

I snatched a couple of pizza rolls from the tray and stuffed them in my mouth. "Bye, troll. Tell Mom I stopped by."

"I'm serious about the DNA thing, Jrue!" she called out.

"You got DNA test money?"

She rolled her brown eyes skyward. "Why do you think I'm asking you?"

"C'mon, this is for my education! Don't you want me to be educated like my big sis?" she asked, hip-bumping me.

"Ask Mom," I insisted while smacking my lips.

"She's not gonna pay for it. C'mon, the commercial said there's a deal like, buy one get one half off or something."

"You think because I'm grown, I got money to spend on anything, huh? I know you know my apartment flooded. Yara and I just moved today."

"Sounds like this is the perfect start for you. New place, new... I don't know."

A quick no jerked my neck. "Yeah, you're doing a terrible job of selling this."

Charity sighed. "All I'm saying is, think about it, 'kay?" she said, patting my back.

"If I get this, don't ask me for a birthday gift or Christmas. Nothing else."

A smile stretched across her cocoa-brown face. "Deal."

Eighteen

KAS

THE BELL chimed against the glass as I sailed through the cafe door to meet with Cena for lunch. The time had come for her to cash in her raincheck for canceling once before, so I had no choice but to honor it. It had been forty-eight hours since I'd felt Jrue's lips against mine, and I was fiending for more of her time and attention. As much as I didn't want to, I pushed my thoughts of her to the back of my mind when I approached the table. A trace of a smile brushed her lips when Cena's eyes caught mine.

"Hey."

"What's up?" I asked before taking my seat across from her.

"Thanks for meeting with me."

I dipped my chin in a nod. "It's no problem."

Silence hung between us, and I immediately focused on whatever was going on in my phone while we waited for the waitress to greet us.

"So, I'm meeting with the planner and her team again in a few days. And I finally settled on a dress. Well, two. One for the ceremony and another for the reception. Everyone is getting excited again, and I'm over here like, *wow, this is really fucking happening,* y'know? I guess it's something about weddings that make people all bubbly inside, but it's all starting to become real for me." Cena babbled.

"Yeah," I muttered, not bothering to tear my eyes away from Jrue's Instagram page.

"Have you done your fitting for your tux yet?"

I shook my head. "Nah. What about you? You got your dress yet?"

She rolled her eyes and sighed. "I literally *just* told you I did."

My brows creased in confusion before her comment registered in my head. "What? Oh–oh damn, my fault. Sorry."

"Look, Kas. I know you're a busy man, and we're only doing this for our families, but I would ask that you give me the respect of your time while I'm in your presence," she stated.

She couldn't have come across as more straightforward. Her words prompted me to put my phone down and flip it over on the table. "I'm sorry. You're right. I think I spent so much time rebelling against the idea, but the more I fight it, the closer we seem to get to it."

"I just want to clarify that I know exactly what this is. I don't want anything from you. I'm not delusional, and I'm not expecting to fall in love. But what I am expecting is for you to fall in line. I wrapped my head around the whole concept of doing what I had to do for my family a long time ago. You'd be wise to do the same."

I scoffed before blurting out, "This sounds like it means just as much to you as it does to my father."

"Why? Because he wants to expand?"

My brows raised. "How'd *you* know about that?"

"I know a lot more than anyone thinks I do, Kas. But what I promise you no one knows is that *I'm* the one that's in line to get my father's seat when he steps down."

My eyebrows flashed up. "What?"

"Yeah, exactly. Everyone thinks it's going to be my brother Canaan because he's *'the favorite'* and I'm just *'Daddy's princess.'* But my father has been grooming me to take his place for years. He told me that's what he wants, and it's in his will. Our marriage is just a tiny piece of a much bigger puzzle," she informed me.

AN HOUR LATER, I left my lunch date with Cena with more information than I had bargained for. She went on and on about how incompetent her twin brother was, but no matter how many mistakes he made, her father would always forgive him, proving what I already knew to be true about him. She'd indeed surprised me in a good way, and I'd enjoyed my time more than I thought I would. She was insightful and clever, reminding me never to underestimate a woman, especially not one with a thirst for power. On my way to the building, I called Kamil to tell him the news, but it rang until his voicemail picked up. I shot him a quick text the minute I parked. I hopped out of the car to see Jrue parked across the street with a sandwich glued to her lips.

I sauntered up to her window and tapped my knuckle against it. She jumped before huffing out a piece of lettuce at the steering wheel. She cut her eyes at me. "What the fuck!" she yelled from behind the glass. "You scared the shit out of me!"

"I'm sorry." I laughed. "Yo, you should've seen your face."

She rolled down the window. "That's not funny at all."

"Where you going?"

"I was just headed out to look for some pieces for the lobby. It's almost done, but I'm looking for something."

"What are you looking for?"

"I'll know when I find it."

"You, uh, you want some company?" I inquired.

Her right brow arched. "Yeah? You don't have big business boss man stuff to handle in there?"

I shook my head. "Nah."

"Cool. Hop in," she insisted while unlocking the doors.

"Where are we going anyway?" I asked once we pulled off.

"Thrifting."

"What the fuck is that?"

She giggled. "Careful. Your privilege is showing."

I laughed back. "Shut up."

"I thought you might wanna see where your money was going."

After a thirty-minute drive across the city, she announced we'd made it to our destination. My brows creased when I studied my surroundings. We were in the thrift store parking lot. "You gon' put shit from a thrift store in the lobby of my luxury condos?"

"Relax. Full creative control, remember?"

"If I go in here, you gotta be able to handle my honesty. If I don't like that shit, it's gotta go," I declared.

"Part of me being able to do my job means you being able to trust me."

"Do you trust me?"

"No, do you trust me?" she asked before killing the engine.

"No," I replied.

She winked. "Good."

I watched Jrue leaf through a stack of artwork leaning against the wall and pour over mismatched throw pillows, chandeliers, rugs, and other used knickknacks. After an hour of pushing through narrow aisles, blocked by people with rattling wheels on their shopping carts, we exited through the automatic doors. The minute we stepped outside, the big canvas tents and amusement rides at the other end of the parking lot caught her eye.

"What's going on down there?"

"Looks like a carnival. They've got half the lot blocked off down there for it."

"I used to love the carnival growing up," she informed me.

"Yeah?"

She bobbed her head up and down. "Oh yeah. Man, the funnel cakes, the candy apples, the rides... the Ferris wheel was always my favorite. Y'know, right?"

I wagged my head in a no. "Nah. I don't, actually."

Her brows raised. "You mean to tell me you've never been to a carnival before?"

I swayed my head again. "Nope."

She grabbed my arm. "That settles it. We're going."

"Nah. I don't have time for that today."

"I thought you said you didn't have any big boss man shit to do today?"

"I know what I said, but—"

"But nothing. We're going. We're walking. Let's go!"

I allowed her to drag me along, enjoying the view of her body in that sundress as she forged ahead of me. It hugged her curves in all the right places, curves I wouldn't mind steering my hands around again. Ever since we kissed at her apartment, we'd been a mixture of close and distant. We kept it professional in the building, but I always wanted to sneak to kiss her cheek or grab her hand when no one was looking.

The smell of buttery popcorn, hotdogs, and cotton candy wafted past my nostrils as we made our way past the food and game vendors heckling us to spend our money on their corndogs, pretzels, and ring toss games. We inched deeper into the carnival, surveying all it had to offer. I spent the rest of the afternoon riding the bumper cars and letting her win at different shooting target games.

"He's so cute." Jrue gushed as she toted around the oversized stuffed bear that I'd won her.

"That jawn aight."

"I'm ready for that funnel cake now, though. You ever had one?"

"Nah, but I got you."

Once she had her warm funnel cake in hand, I watched her pick apart a piece before slicing her teeth into it. "Mmm. This is what Heaven tastes like. I'm sure of it. You want a bite?"

"Nah. You enjoy it."

"You sure I can't tempt you with a piece of this delicious, warm, sweet funnel cake? You don't know what you're missing." She enticed me before sucking the powdered sugar from her fingertips.

I smirked. "Only for you, I'll break my diet."

Jrue pulled apart a piece and landed it inside my mouth. "Good, right?" she asked, watching me chew.

"Hell yeah. This jawn is good as a mothafucka."

A smile dominated her face before she went over to sit on a wide hay bale. "Come sit and help me finish this because it's not going home with me."

"You've got a little something on your, uh—"

"What? What is it?"

"Powdered sugar on your nose. Here, I got you," I announced, inching closer before gently swiping it away. "There, perfect."

"Can I ask you something?" she asked before feeding me another piece of funnel cake.

"Can I say no?"

"No."

"Then ask away."

"How is it that you're single? You're handsome, successful…"

"You're single, too, right?" I interjected.

"Yeah."

"I could be asking you the same thing. You're beautiful, talented…"

"And a Scorpio." She cut me off. "You already know I enjoy my me time."

"I get it. Now I've got a question," I stated.

"Yeah?"

"You remember the day you moved and asked me all those questions. You asked me somethin' like, tell me the story of your first love."

"What about it?"

"Tell me yours," I insisted.

She turned her face away from me. "Trust me; you don't wanna hear about that."

"Why don't I?"

Jrue shrugged her shoulders. "Because there's nothing to tell. I haven't been in anything serious in a—a long time."

"Why not?"

"Just wasn't meant to be, I guess."

"What makes something meant to be for you?" I inquired, eyeing her closely as I awaited her reply.

"The love has to feel like nineties RnB. If it doesn't, then I don't want it."

"What do you mean by that?"

"I don't know; I guess I've always been kind of an old soul at heart. Like, If I'm in a relationship with you and we beefin', I don't want an apology through text. I don't wanna talk it out over FaceTime. I want a sincere, to my face, slow jam, I'm sorry mixtape type of apology."

"Oh, so you wanna nigga down on bended knee and shit?" I chuckled.

She playfully punched my arm. "Exactly! I enjoy the tradition of being courted and wooed and made to feel special instead of being made to feel like a piece of ass."

"So, you wanna be married one day? Kids and all that?"

"Yeah, why not? If I find the one, I wouldn't mind spending the rest of my life with that person."

"Do you have a type?"

"Why? You tryna find me a date?" she joked. "You know the grand opening mixer is only a few weeks away."

I dipped my chin. "Yeah, I know."

I hadn't put much thought into a date for my own event, nor had I entertained the idea of seeing Jrue on another man's arm in my presence. As badly as I wanted to tell her she was mine and that I would waste any nigga she brought around me, I didn't. I couldn't. I wanted her so fuckin' bad, and yet I talked myself off the edge every time I thought about saying or doing something I'd regret. I was like a ticking time bomb around her. Before I could drum up something witty about finding her a date, she sprung to her feet to toss the plate in a nearby trashcan.

"You haven't had the complete carnival experience unless you ride the Ferris wheel. It's like a carnival staple!" she voiced.

I stood to my feet while swiping the hay from my pants. "Fine. Let's do it."

The paint-chipped safety bar rested tightly across our laps as we sat on the Ferris wheel. Her thighs rubbed against mine like a cat brushing up against their owner's leg. The warm breeze sailed through her hair, causing her curls to blow across her face. "Thanks for this. It was fun," I told her.

She flashed me a warm smile. "Hey, you'd never experienced the feel of pillowy soft cotton candy melting in your mouth or what it feels like to kiss someone at the top of the Ferris wheel. It was only right I took your V-card," she said with a soft chuckle.

"So, you've kissed someone at the top of a Ferris wheel before?" I inquired.

She shook her head. "Well, no, but—"

Our lips met amongst the spinning rides and flashing lights, placing a pause on her sentence. The warmth of her body washed against mine, slamming into me like a cool ocean wave. Our fingers slowly twined together, drawing us even closer. Time seemed to stop as I pressed my forehead against hers and pulled away from her lips, only to return for more seconds later. I knew I shouldn't have laid one finger on her, tasted her lips, or allowed her to invade my thoughts, but she'd already gotten under my skin.

Jrue remained tucked in my arms for the remainder of the ride before we drifted back across the parking lot to her car, fingers tangled in one another's. I didn't want to let her go. My mind searched for any reason to keep the vibe right where it was.

"Hey, so, um, I think I'm lookin' to redecorate my spot. You think that's something you'd be willing to take on once you're done with the building?"

She dipped her chin in agreement. "Oh, most definitely. What exactly is your vision for your place?"

I twisted my neck to hers as we approached her car. "You wanna see it?"

"When? Now?"

I jerked my chin in agreement. "Yeah. Sure. If you want. That way, you can give me some ideas."

"My ideas aren't free, so expect a bill after tonight," she joked. "Yeah, no. That's cool. Once I wrap with the building, I'd be happy to talk next steps."

"Next steps, huh?" I asked, tilting her chin upward to kiss her again. Jrue smirked. "You're dangerous, y'know that?"

I stole another kiss before responding. "More than you know."

"Oh, I bet."

"So, you down to come to my place and check out the space?"

"Yeah."

"Bet. Maybe we can order in for dinner, or I'll call up one of my chefs and have him make us something," I offered.

"You spent all day with me, and now you're talking about dinner? Are you always this damn charming?"

"What can I say? A nigga likes to eat," I said, eyeing her devilishly. "Give me the keys. I'll drive."

Nineteen

JRUE

I CLENCHED my thighs together the entire ride to Kas's place. He just didn't know how sexy he was. Or maybe he did. Either way, I wanted him *badly*. I'd spent most of the day in his presence, soaking in everything about him. He'd recently started trying out a vegan lifestyle. He worked out religiously each morning at six o'clock; politically, he was more Malcolm than Martin. Aside from that, I liked who he was around me and vice versa. It was the first time in a long time I felt like I could be myself. I hadn't smiled or laughed that hard in a while. Hell, I hadn't allowed anyone to get remotely close to me since Darius was killed. At least not on an emotional level. And yet, we'd shared a perfect day. Letting him hit would just be the icing on the cake.

We pulled up to his building, and I realized he lived in one of Philly's most top-tier residences. The minute we stepped inside the private elevator, he crashed his lips into mine. The ding from his private floor elevator pried us apart before the doors opened to his spacious two-story penthouse. The ceilings were elevated, and the floors were marble.

"Wow. This is *really* nice," I commented while examining his private space with the most amazing views of the city I'd ever seen.

"It's alright."

"You realize you've seen where I live, right? Stop trying to downplay this!" I stated while proceeding on my self-guided tour.

Top-of-the-line appliances and quartz countertops graced his modern kitchen. The expansive windows infused natural light into the spacious living room and a covered terrace where his Peloton bike was stationed. Down the main hall were the dining room and den garnished with high-end modern finishings. The master and guest rooms were stationed upstairs on the second floor. Everything about his bedroom *screamed* masculinity. From the custom onyx marble floors to the sleek, satin bedding and the black, abstract artwork adorning each wall.

"You like what you see?" he asked, leaning his broad shoulder against the doorframe.

"It's dark, but it's nice."

"It's my favorite room in the entire place."

"Why? Because this is the bed where you fuck?" I quipped.

An adventurous grin spread across his face. "I don't need a bed to fuck. Do you?"

My heart rate accelerated, and my thoughts began to pop like bubbles, one by one. All my words got trapped inside my throat, and my brain short-circuited. We weren't even touching, but my heart was going crazy.

A sly smirk lifted one corner of his lips. "Well, do you?"

I swallowed hard before shaking my head. "No."

"Good," he responded before inching up my dress and slipping his hand between my warm thighs.

I paused my breath as his fingertips teased my inner thigh. A moan escaped my lips when he pressed his thumb against my clit. I was *aching* to be touched. We both knew it. Kas locked his hand behind the back of my neck and pulled my lips onto his.

"I've been dreaming of this," he whispered against my lips between kisses. "How good your pussy would feel clenching my dick."

"Mmm."

"How loud you'd moan when I'm fuckin' the shit outta you," he continued.

My knees went limp, causing me to clutch his waist. I clawed at his flesh while whimpering for him not to stop. Kas ran his hand over my breasts before pulling down my strap and flicking his long tongue against my nipple. The more I moaned, the faster and harder he rubbed my clit.

"Oh! Oh shit! Don't stop!" I begged.

Kas pressed his lips against my ear. "Mmm, or how many times I could make you squirt all over this dick." He mumbled before lifting me into his arms and pressing my back against the nearest wall. My fingertips roamed all over his bearded face as I sucked his tongue. With my legs enveloping his waist, he continued to finger fuck me.

"Oooh shit! Yes! Yes!" I squealed, climaxing just as his doorbell chimed.

My eyes popped wide to see him staring back at me. He watched me cum in real time, and we couldn't tear our eyes away from each other. "Mmm. Those sexy ass thighs are shaking so much."

My hips twitched with excitement and arousal, ready for the main course, when the doorbell sounded again.

He sighed. "Give me a minute to see who it is."

Kas pressed a few kisses against my collarbone before putting me down. He walked over to his bedside and tapped a few buttons against a tablet before looking at me. "It's my father. He's trying to come up. Let me go handle him."

"Okay. No problem. I'm, um, I'm going to use your bathroom," I told him.

"Okay. I'll be right back."

I tipped my head forward before sailing inside his master bath. The second the door closed behind me, I rested my back against it for a few seconds, trying to come down from the high I was on. He had me seeing stars off his fingers alone, so I *knew* the dick would have me dizzy. After a minute, my eyes scanned the space. Like his bedroom, everything in his bathroom was damn near black too. Black subway tile graced every wall, and the light fixture above the vanity mirror, showerhead, faucet, and cabinet handles were all chrome gold. I rested my elbows against the marble countertop before splashing water against my face. I needed to cool off. My head was spinning, and I was wide open and wetter than a tropical storm. Had the doorbell not rung, he would've probably been balls deep inside me.

Kas had my panties soaked and my juices dripping down my inner thigh. I quickly hoisted my sundress over my hips and peeled them off. I'd planned to bury them inside my purse before I realized I'd left it on the kitchen counter during my tour.

"Shit." I grumbled before balling them tightly in my fists.

I pushed my dirty thoughts aside and came out of the bathroom, only to hear yelling from downstairs. I crept over to the open bedroom door and midway down the stairs before my eyes landed on Kas and his father in the middle of a heated discussion.

"I shouldn't have to remind you of your responsibilities as the next in line to head this family!"

"You think I don't know that?" Kas answered.

"Then what are you doing, Kasim?"

"Nothing. It's nothing. I have everything under control. I know my limits."

"You know what you need to start putting your effort into, not whatever this is."

"You said what you had to say. Now can you please go," Kas stated as more of a demand than a question, ushering his father to the elevator doors.

The minute his finger tapped the button, he twisted his neck and saw me. "Sorry, I was, uh, just looking for my purse," I announced to them both.

His father cut his eyes at me, softening his gaze after a few seconds. "And you are?"

Kas interjected, "Pa, this is Jrue. Jrue, this is my father, Julius."

I dipped my chin. "Nice to meet you."

"She's been doing the interior design work for the condos downtown. We were going over plans for her to redesign some things here," Kas continued.

I plastered a fake smile across my face while nodding in agreement. Minutes before his father showed up, he had his tongue halfway down my throat. Yet, in the presence of company, I had been reduced to *just* the designer. I was a little in my feelings that I didn't receive a more formal introduction, but then again, I didn't have a clear idea of what the hell we were doing. Up until minutes prior, we'd only kissed.

Julius smiled politely before turning his attention back to his son as the elevator dinged. "Nice meeting you, Jrue," he replied before stepping inside and shooting his son a look before the metal doors closed.

"I thought I told you I'd be right back," Kas said, turning his eyes to mine.

I nodded. "I know, but I wanted to slide these in my purse and realized I left it down here," I informed him while dangling my panties in his face.

He snatched them from me before sliding them into his pocket. "Where were we?"

"You tell me. What was that about?" I pointed to the elevator.

His brows snapped together. "What do you mean?"

"I mean, you were just upstairs finger fucking the shit out of me, and then you introduced me to your family like I was a stranger. Like, what did I just walk into?"

"Nothing. It's nothing. He should've never even gotten the chance to see you, that's all."

"Why not?"

He shook his head, visibly frustrated. "It's nothing. Can we drop it?"

"No. Tell me what you meant by that. What? I'm good enough to work for you but not good enough to meet your father. Is that it?" I accused.

"You don't know what you're talking about. That's not what I'm saying at all."

"Then what are you sayin', Kas?"

He stared at me with a blank look on his face. After an ominous silence, I turned toward the elevator door. "You know what, this whole thing was stupid. I shouldn't have thought that we... I—I just thought —nothing, never mind. I gotta go," I stated.

He held his hand out to stop me. "No, say it. You thought what?"

"I think by now it's pretty obvious, but I'm feeling the shit outta you, Kas. And up until now, I thought it was mutual, but maybe it's not. And if so, then that's my bad. I can keep things professional; just let me know how *you* want to roll," I stated, putting the ball in his court.

Kas pushed out a deep sigh before running his hand down his beard. "You know what? We *should* keep things professional."

I tried my best to keep my jaw wired shut and, instead, hit him with a nod before making my way into the kitchen to retrieve my purse. There was no way he would get an argument out of me. I'd already made it clear how open he had me. There was nothing left to say except, "Got it."

I jabbed at the elevator button, and the doors spread apart seconds later. Kas didn't even try to stop me. He only stood there, frozen by the stairs, as if I'd pressed pause on a movie. I huffed out a loud sigh when the elevator started to glide down. Our chemistry was undeniable, or at least to me it was, but if that was what he wanted, I could put on my big girl pants and stop things dead in their tracks. The next time I laid eyes on Kasim Barnes, it would be all business, *zero* pleasure.

Back inside my car, I fumbled with my keys before turning on the ignition. Instead of hearing the purr I'd been accustomed to, the engine spat and sputtered, refusing to start.

"No. Hell no! Not here! Not right now!" I groaned, trying the engine again to no avail. "Fuck!" I screamed while taking out my frustrations on the steering wheel. "What the fuck am I gonna do now?"

I shuffled around my purse until I pulled out my phone to call Yara. Before I could tap her name, I heard tapping against my window. "Listen, I'm sorry about what happened up there," Kas stated. "Can we talk?"

My neck swayed. "No. I'm good. I'm going home."

"It doesn't look like this jawn tryna take you there, but I can get you home."

"I don't need your help!" I heard him suck his perfect teeth while I tried the engine a third time for good luck. Nothing happened. "Goddammit!"

I tore my attention back to my phone and noticed my battery had less than ten percent. Either I would call Yara and wait for her while Kas attempted to plead his case, or I could risk what was left of my battery to call an Uber.

"Yo, Jrue. Open the door," he said, tapping at the glass. I kept my neck stationed forward before Kas bent down to station his glare right at me. "I said open the door!"

"Trust me, I'm good. You made your point, aight? Now leave me alone. I'll be out of your way as soon as my Uber gets here," I assured him.

"You don't have to call an Uber. I'll take you home and get your car towed to my mechanic's shop."

"Didn't you hear me say I'm good?"

"Why you always actin' so independent and shit? If I said I'll help, I'll help. Get out the car."

"And have to listen to you run your mouth all the way back to my spot? No. I'm good!" I yelled through the window.

"Fuckouttahere, yo! I swear to God, you're the most stubborn person I've ever met in my life! I'm not chasing you!"

I snapped my neck at him. He had me on ten. I popped open the driver's side door and hopped out on his ass. "Why are you still talkin' to me, huh? I told you I'm getting a ride. Go back inside to your perfect little high-maintenance, privileged life!" I pointed.

"Oh, I see. You think a nigga livin' on easy street because you got to see where I lay my head at night, and you see me makin' the moves that I *allow* you to see. You got your mind made up about me already."

"That's not true. I'm just saying—"

"If shit were sweet, I wouldn't have to war with my family about who the fuck I can—you know what, never mind. Fuck it! Believe what you want about me. It's easier that way," he concluded, tossing up his hands.

"Wait. War with your family? About what?" I quizzed, wanting him to dial it back.

He shook his head, unwilling to continue the conversation. "Nothing. Never mind. Forget I fuckin' said anything. Do you want a ride home or not? I'm not gon' ask again, Jrue."

I shifted my weight from one leg to the other, weighing it against the other zero options I had at my disposal. I glanced down at my phone that was on eight percent, and finally nodded. "Yeah. Um, thanks..."

Twenty

YARA

THE SWEET SMELL of sugar and melted butter traveled past my nose as I stepped up to the glass bakery counter. My stomach grumbled as I looked vacantly at the trays of glistening donuts, bagels, muffins, and more sweet treats on display. After deciding on an apple danish and a coffee, the cash register dinged. I placed the danish on top of my laptop and carried my cup of coffee in the other hand before taking my seat at an empty table. The crunch of the sweet bread rattled against my teeth as I dusted the crumbs off my fingertips before cracking open my laptop. Seconds later, my cell rang, and Blake's name popped up on the screen.

My eyes rolled before I pressed accept. "Yes, Blake?" I answered.

"Are you there?"

"Yup, waiting on the client to show."

She pulled the phone away to cough before sniffling. "Okay, good."

"Don't worry, I got this," I assured her.

"Don't forget to get the shot list. The photographer has been asking for us to send it over."

"Yup, got it. Oop! Gotta go. She's here." I licked the sugary glaze from my lips before standing to greet her. "Thanks for meeting with me on such short notice. Blake is down with the flu, but she wanted to ensure I got everything in order for your review."

"No problem," Cena said, taking her seat across from me.

"Your big day is fast approaching! How do you feel? Are you excited?"

"Um, yeah, I guess."

I swiped a napkin at my lips before getting started. "Alright, let's get down to it. Um, let's see. Have you two decided if you'll be saying your own vows?"

Her head fluttered from left to right. "I hadn't thought about it."

"It's something you may want to consider, but there's nothing wrong with going along with the officiant. Weddings are emotional events, after all."

"I don't think ours will be."

"Why not?"

"It's just not our thing."

"Okay. That's not a problem. Um, oh. Blake also wanted me to remind you to secure your marriage license if you two haven't already done so."

"Got it."

"And did you have a chance to work on the shot list for me to send all your must-have pictures to the photographer?"

"Yes. It's in my email draft. I'll send it over now. Let me know when you get it," she said, clicking away at her phone.

I refreshed my email and opened her message. "Got it. Okay, let's see what we've got here. The groom and his family members; father, Julius; brother, Kamil; the bride with her family members; father, Silas; brother, Ca—" I paused, breath hitching in my throat.

I silently scanned Canaan's name over and over, unsure if there was a connection between the Canaan McQueen in the email and the Canaan Mitchell I was fucking. Philly was a large city, and Canaan wasn't an uncommon name, but I couldn't shake the feeling that something wasn't right.

"Is everything okay?"

I cleared my throat. "Y-yeah. Yup, okay. This looks good. I'll get this over to the photographers today."

"Okay, great."

"Actually, I do have one question. I see you have your brother

Canaan listed, but I don't think we have his photo on the wedding party page for your website. Would you happen to have a photo you can send to me so that we can get that added?"

"Uh, yeah, sure. One second. Let me see if I have anything in my phone."

We sat silently for a few minutes, listening to the low buzz of conversation around us. "How about this one? Will this work?" she asked, flipping her screen to me.

My eyes lit up with surprise as I stared at a photo of Canaan, and my wheels began to churn. When we met, he told me his last name was Mitchell. I knew the only time a man lied about his last name was if he were married or trying to scam a bitch. We hadn't spoken to each other since the last time I left his apartment. By then, we both knew it was over. What was the point in confronting him now? It wouldn't change a damn thing. I was done with him and focusing all my attention on Nate and making our marriage work. Before forcing a smile, I shook my head to get my thoughts back in order. "Yup. That's perfect. Thank you. I know I went over quite a lot, but is there anything else you wanted to discuss today? Don't hold back on me. This is your special day, and we want to ensure your wedding day runs as smoothly as possible."

Cena's smile displayed a full grid of white teeth. "No, you've been great. Thank you. Sorry if it seems like I'm spacing out. I've just got a lot on my mind."

"That's to be expected. Planning a wedding takes a village. And with that, I do want to let you know that we have all your vendor contracts taken care of, but I'm going to go through and double-check all the details with a fine-tooth comb before our next check-in on the seventeenth," I assured her before closing my laptop.

"You mean the twenty-seventh?" she quizzed.

I reluctantly swung my head before swiping to view the calendar on my phone. I'd been working so hard helping Blake crank out one happily ever after, after another, that I hadn't taken more than a few minutes a day to slow down and focus on myself. If I had, I would've known my period was a week and a half late.

I sucked in a sharp breath. "You're right. That's my fault. Yup, the twenty-seventh."

Cena got up from the table, the diamond on her finger shining as she waved and walked away. I remained seated, mind too stuck on the fact that I'd missed my period and hadn't even noticed. *Maybe it's stress,* I thought. It *was* wedding season, and I had been working my ass off. The thought of being pregnant made my legs feel like Jell-O. There was no way. No fuckin' way that I could be pregnant. I swiped to open my period tracker app and went back to the last few times I'd had sex with Canaan and Nate. It had been weeks for both, but Canaan was my last.

"Fuck," I mumbled before finding the strength to get up.

I looked at my half-eaten Danish, and I felt sick. I gathered my things in a hurry and bustled through the door. I knew I had an old pregnancy test in my bathroom cabinet, so I hurried home to take it. I continued to guzzle my lukewarm coffee all the way home to ensure my bladder was ready to burst by the time I arrived.

"Jrue? Are you home!" I yelled as I walked through the door.

Silence greeted me as I charged down the hallway, ready to tell her how badly I'd fucked up. Her vacant room was proof that I was alone. My legs marched into my bathroom as if I was going in for a death sentence. My thirst for pleasure had formed the love triangle from hell; if the test was positive, life as I knew it would be over. I wished there was *no way* I could've been carrying Canaan's baby, but we weren't always one hundred percent safe, but that was what the fuck birth control was supposed to be for. If I could've, I would've kicked my own ass. It was clear Canaan was a liar and couldn't be trusted. As good as the dick was, it wasn't worth a baby. A million and one thoughts continued to race through my head as I waited for the test results. My timer dinged after three minutes just as my phone dinged with a text from Nate. I ignored it while drawing in a tight breath and slamming my eyes shut before looking down at the stick.

My eyelids unfastened, and all the air flew right out of my lungs like a balloon that had been deflated. "Oh fuck," I mouthed in silence.

On the edge of the sink was a positive test staring back at me. Rattled as all hell, I scrolled to my unopened text to read Nate's message.

Nate: *Can't wait to see you this weekend, bae.*

Twenty-One

KAS

AS PROMISED, I had Jrue's car towed to my mechanic, repaired, and returned to her within a few days. After that, I spent the next week and a half avoiding her. She'd almost completed the entire project, yet time couldn't move fast enough. The further apart we were, the better off we'd both be. At least that was what I kept telling myself every time I looked her way or smelled the reminiscent of her fragrance long after she'd left the room. I couldn't believe I had her right in my arms and let her slip away. I was still pissed that my father was even able to lay eyes on her. She thought it was because I didn't think she was good enough. She couldn't have been further from the truth. I wanted to keep her away from everything about my family, *The Order*, and how I really made my money. Jrue didn't need to know that side of me. But the only way I could ensure that was by staying the fuck away from her. I snapped out of my thoughts when my phone dinged with a text from Cena.

Cena: *Will you be here soon? We need to talk.*

Me: *Yeah. Be there in ten.*

I parked outside her family's art gallery, still mentally trying to get my head in the game. Once inside, I spotted Cena standing near the front desk with tear-stained eyes.

"What's up? Why you crying?" I asked, approaching her side.

"Let's go to the back."

She slid her hand into mine, and I followed her to the back office and closed the door behind me. "What's wrong?" I asked.

"It's my—father. He-he's dying."

"What?"

Fresh tears slid down her face. The ring on her finger glistened as she swiped her left hand across her face. "Cancer. Stage four. His doctors are saying he has six months at best," she announced, voice trembling.

I swiped my hand down my face, covering my shock. "Oh shit. I'm sorry to hear that."

She dipped her chin in a nod. "Yeah. Me too."

I instinctively reached out to pull her into a hug, allowing her to wet my Dior shirt with her sorrows. "What do you need from me?" I asked.

She raised her eyes to mine. "We need to move up the wedding, Kas."

My brows rose, then fell. "To when?"

"From a couple of months to a few weeks. Can you be okay with that?"

I nodded reluctantly. "Yeah. Whatever you need."

She let out a long sigh, letting me know she'd been holding her breath, awaiting my response. "Thank you."

I left the art gallery with my phone pressed to my ear. When I slammed my body into the driver's seat, I had Kamil on the other line.

"What's good, ak?" he answered.

I sailed past his greeting and barreled right into my burning question. "Does Pa know Silas McQueen is dying?"

The line fell silent for a few seconds before Kamil responded, "Oh shit..."

"He's got stage four cancer."

"How long he got?"

"Cena said six months at best. She just found out."

"Damn, yo. That's crazy."

"I know, but that ain't all."

"What?"

"Because of his condition, she wants to move up the wedding to a few weeks."

"Oh shit. What did you say?"

"What else could I say? Her fuckin' father is dying, Mil."

"I know, I know. But, damn. You ready?"

"I don't have any other choice."

"Well, look on the bright side," he suggested.

"What bright side?"

"Shit, I don't know. I was hoping you would jump in that jawn with something," he confessed.

I smacked my teeth. "Fuckouttahere, man."

"I'm sorry, yo. I'm sorry. Aight, in all seriousness and shit, you good?"

"Again, what other choice is there?" I asked before huffing out a stale sigh.

The more I pushed against it, the more the universe slammed it back in my face. I had to wrap my mind around the harsh reality that anything between Jrue and me would never come to fruition.

Twenty-Two

JRUE

RAIN PELTED the glass as heavy gray clouds blocked out the sunlight, dulling the view of the city from the living room condo. I was done looking for things to fix or spruce up so I could justify staying around any longer. As badly as I was ready to be through with Kasim Barnes, I wanted everything to be perfect. This project was my name-sake. Lightning flashes lit up the clouds, and the earth rumbled as I punched the elevator button. The doors opened, revealing Kas standing inside the metal box. My knees locked, and my heart thudded in my chest.

"H-hey," I stammered while stepping in.

He moved to the back, leaning his shoulder against the wall. "'Sup?"

I kept my chin tucked toward my chest as I hit the ground button. "Heading out," I answered.

"Did you, um, meet with the photographer?" Kas asked, making conversation.

"From marketing? Yes. He sent over the proofs to my email about an hour ago. I haven't looked at them yet."

"I'm sure they're fine."

"Yeah."

"So, everything is ready for the mixer on Saturday?"

I ducked my chin in agreement before allowing my eyes to drift up to his and instantly regretted it. "Yeah."

He glanced at me before turning his attention to his phone. It was clear he had other things on his mind. "Cool."

I couldn't have been more grateful to see the numbers winding down until the elevator dinged. As soon as the doors parted wide enough for me to slip through, I did.

"Jrue, wait up—" Kas called out from behind me.

I held up my hand to stop him as more storm clouds boiled across the sky. "I gotta go."

"Jrue—"

"It's storming. I gotta get home," I insisted.

He stared at me, and I instantly felt ill. It was almost as if he was looking right through me. I twisted on my heels and skated toward the door. It stung to walk away, but I had to deal with it. As much as I may have hated his mysterious ass, he was good in my book as long as the check cleared.

WHEN I GOT HOME, I was shocked to discover that I hadn't returned to an empty place. Yara was in the kitchen making tacos and Spanish rice for dinner.

A grin stretched across my lips. "Well, isn't this a pleasant surprise?"

"I thought I'd make you a meal since I haven't seen you in forever."

I set my bag down on the counter. "Yeah, the place was really starting to lose its domestic vibe."

"Yeah, I bet. I haven't seen you pick up a spatula since we moved here," she joked.

"But seriously, friend. How the hell are you? It's been weeks since I laid eyes on you. I was beginning to forget I had a roommate."

"I know, right? I'm coming. You're going. Or the other way around. But life has been... a lot, to say the least."

"Everything okay?" I asked, arching a questioning brow.

"Y-yeah," she stammered. "I've just been working nonstop. You know me, a busy bee."

"Yeah, I see you've been super busy."

"You remember the wedding I told you about with the big-ass budget?"

"What about it?"

Yara flinched when the boom of thunder hit. "Damnit, I hate thunderstorms!"

I laughed as the strong winds whipped the trees back and forth. "Why are you so scary?"

"Shut up! If I weren't standing in this apartment right now, your ass would be in the fetal position under the covers."

My eyes rolled skyward. "Can we get back to the wedding with the big ass budget, please?"

"Fine. They pushed up the wedding because the bride's father is sick or something."

"Aww, damn."

"Right, so sad. But, what we may have had weeks to plan, we now have what seems like days for this to still be the five-hundred-thousand-dollar dream wedding she's paying for." Yara huffed.

"Wow. That's crazy."

"Girl, the cake alone was five thousand dollars. There are five hundred people on their guest list. This wedding will be the event of the season, darling!"

"I know this means a bigger payday for you, right?"

"Hell yeah. Rush job means rush money. Christmas has come early! At this point, I'll sleep when I'm dead. What about you? How's your project going with WorkBae?"

"Ugh. When are you going to stop calling him that? Nothing is going on between us... anymore."

"Hold up. Anymore? Why was I not informed that anything started in the first place?" Yara inquired with her brows raised.

"Because there was nothing to tell. We kissed a couple of times and then agreed that we needed to keep things professional."

"Because you're working together, right?"

I bobbed my head. "Yeah. Right."

"Shouldn't you be wrapping up your project soon? It's been some months."

I tilted my head in a yes for a second time. "Yeah. The grand opening mixer is less than a week away, and that's that."

"So..."

"So, what?"

"What happens after that? Will WorkBae become RealBae? Find out on the next episode of *Jrue's Twisted Love Life*," Yara joked.

"You're a whole ass clown. Y'know that?" I asked with an eye roll.

"I'm just saying. I know I told you to keep it tight and keep your professional hat on, but the project is about to be over. If the attraction is there, why not?"

"That's the thing. I'm not sure it is there anymore."

"What do you mean?"

I shrugged. "I don't know. He's this beautiful, sexy, charismatic, gentle, protective creature. He's caring and calm. He makes such boss moves in a wave of silence. He's spontaneous like me, and I know the sex would be *fucking epic.*"

Yara interjected. "I'm not seeing the problem here."

"But on the other hand, he's got this hard exterior shell, and the minute you think you cracked off a piece, something even harder grows back in its place. And he's secretive."

"How so?"

"I know he's hiding something, but I don't know what it is."

"Have you asked him?"

"We're not speaking."

"Why not?"

I huffed, realizing I'd kept all the tea about Kas and me to myself for weeks. "Long story short, we were at his place. Things were going great. The whole day, really. And then, the fuckin' doorbell rang."

"And? What happened then?"

"He answered it."

"Who was it? Another bitch or somethin'?"

My neck fish-tailed from side to side. "No. It was his father. And it was like the minute he saw my face, everything changed."

"How?"

"I can't explain it. It wasn't anything he said but more how he looked and what he didn't say."

"What did you expect him to say?"

"That's the thing. I *don't* know. Like, I know I would've been freaked out if he introduced me as his girlfriend, but the way he introduced me as the designer for his condos made me feel like, oh, so that's it? I'm *just* that to you?"

Yara nodded in agreement. "Yeah. I get it."

"And it's not like we were even at a point where we would put titles on anything, but it was such a vibe, Ya-Ya. I swear our chemistry was just... damn. I've never felt this way before about another nigga, ever."

"So, what you gon' do about it?" she quizzed, her brows snapped together.

I gave her a lazy shrug. "We agreed to be professional. What other choice do I have but to do just that?"

"I guess we'll find out this weekend," she predicted.

"Yeah, I guess we will."

"Oh! Before I forget, you got some mail. I put it on your dresser."

"Okay, thanks. I'm gonna go take a shower."

"Dinner will be done by the time you get out."

"Cool!" I shouted down the hall as I entered my room. On top of a few pieces of junk mail was the DNA kit I'd ordered with Charity. She'd been bugging me to get it, and since mine had finally arrived, I went ahead and cracked it open. After skimming over the directions, I snapped a picture of me collecting the saliva sample and sent it to Charity as a reminder for her to take the test.

Me: *Don't forget to spit in the tube!*

Charity: *You're disgusting, you know that, right?*

Me: *Love you too, sissy pooh!*

Once I sealed the kit, I tossed it inside my purse to mail it off the next day.

Saturday night

THE GRAND OPENING MIXER DAWNED, and the room buzzed with conversations between developers, real estate agents, investors, Philly's upper echelon, and potential buyers. Light appetizers sat on small plates atop the circular cocktail tables spread throughout the lobby. The wait staff circled the crowds, ensuring everyone with an empty hand was served a glass of bubbly champagne. The space grew warm with people wearing sparkling jewelry and expensive watches. Kas and his team had brought all the right people under one roof. I was excited to finally showcase my work and talent to the type of clients I wanted to work with.

My eyes scanned the room, and it didn't take long for me to zero in on Kas. He was dripping in black, wearing a fitted long-sleeved button-up with the first three buttons undone to show off a few of his tattoos. Even with one button unfastened, the black blazer he was wearing clung to his muscles as if it had been painted on. And his ebony slacks left nothing to the imagination. I could see his bulge from across the room. He knew how to make designer look good.

The minute his eyes caught mine, I felt unsteady on my heels. Even from across the room, I could feel his eyes on me. Devouring me. I adjusted the bobby pin scratching my scalp before pulling out a few business cards and tucking my clutch underneath my arm. A few loose curls swayed against the nape of my neck while the rest of my hair was swept into an updo. I could've kicked myself for wearing my hair the way he liked at *his* event. It was like I was practically begging him to notice me. To take my breath away. Anything. I was pathetic, and I knew it. I managed to escape before he could approach me. As good as he looked, I couldn't be bothered with thoughts of what did or didn't happen between us. I had to get my head in the game, work the room, and get myself some business with my freshly printed business cards at the ready.

An hour flew by, and I'd completely run out of all my cards. I knew people came to these events to network and make new connections, and I'd made many of them. After stepping outside for some fresh air, I'd homed in on Kas near the cocktail bar. I'd been wrestling with the part of myself that wanted to thank him for the opportunity and for opening the door for me. I still felt played and was scorned because of it. Amid the back and forth in my head, I found myself inching closer to him when I walked back inside.

"You've been avoiding me all night," Kas declared as soon as I approached his side.

"No, I haven't," I contested. "I've been working."

"I've been watching you."

"I'm aware."

He dragged his eyes up and down my body, drinking me in. "You look beautiful, Jrue."

"Thanks. You look... nice, too." My words were jumbled and as uneven as my breathing.

"I wish you could experience yourself the way other people do."

"What do you mean?"

"Watching every man in here struggle to keep their eyes off you. You've had this entire room in a chokehold since you stepped inside, and you don't even know it."

"Even you?"

"Especially me."

His straightforwardness slayed me, causing me to clear my throat. "Well, um. I came over to say thank you for the opportunity. My inbox is so flooded with business inquiries I might have to hire an assistant."

"It's your talent that got you here, Jrue. I simply opened the door."

I nodded while tearing my eyes down to the cufflinks in his shirt with the letter O on them. "Again, thank you. It was a great opportunity to work on this project."

"The pleasure was all mine."

"Well, goodnight," I stated, turning away from him.

"Stop."

I kept my back turned. "I—"

"We need to talk."

I sighed before twisting my neck to him. "I don't wanna talk because I already know what you're going to say."

"You don't know shit, Jrue. That's your problem."

I smacked my teeth. "And are you finally going to tell me?"

"Not here."

"Then where?" I asked, folding my arms across my chest.

"Come with me."

My heels clicked against the pavement as I followed Kas outside. The minute we stepped around the side of the building, my feelings erupted like a volcano. Everything I'd been holding in for weeks had come to a head and exploded without my consent.

"I don't get anything about you. Not one damn thing. One minute, you say you wanna keep things professional, and the next, you're talking to me and saying things and making me feel things that I know I shouldn't. That I know are a mistake. And yet, after all the time I've spent alone, fighting even the slightest possibility of love, I take one look at you, and I'm a mess. I'm fumbling over myself, trying not to give my heart away to someone who doesn't want it. Doesn't want me," I expelled, pouring out every last ounce of my heart to him.

He reached out to swipe his hand down my cheek gently. "I'd be crazy not to want you, Jrue. That's the fuckin' problem. As much as I want you, I *can't* have you."

"Why not?"

"My life is more complicated than you think."

"How? You never talk about it. You're a walking vault."

"Some secrets should stay secrets. Besides, you wanted professional. I'm giving you that!" he argued.

"We both agreed to keep things professional! Not just me!"

He scoffed. "Yeah. And what good did that do us, huh? Where did that get us? Now we're both stuck with a bunch of fuckin' feelings we can't do shit about."

"Well, the project is done, so we don't have to see each other anymore after tonight."

"There lies another fuckin' problem."

My brows snapped together. "What do you mean?"

"I don't want to not see you again. I—I need you. Your presence. Your laugh. I always need everything about you around me."

The two of us fell silent as if someone had pressed the pause button on our conversation. My heart ticked like an overwound clock. I didn't know what to say. His words had rendered me speechless.

"Say something before I go crazy," he demanded.

"What do you want me to say? First, you play me close, and then you push me away. Now you're standing here telling me you need me, but oh wait, yeah, you can't have me for whatever reason. You're not tired of all this push and pull, Kas? Because I am."

"So, you wanna be done? You wanna walk away and let that be that?"

"Something that never started can't be done," I reminded him.

"Fine. Tell me to walk away, and I'll step."

"No. Don't do that to me, Kas!"

"Do what?"

"Don't suddenly make it seem like now I'm the one with all the power when you still haven't told me why we can't be together!"

"Because I'd body a nigga over you without question!" he roared.

My breath hitched. "Kas—"

He stepped closer, closing the space between us. "The reason I'm watching niggas in a room when you around is to be ready to check them if they step outta line around you. The night I met you and shit popped off at the club, I lost my brother. My fuckin' blood. And as hurt as I was over that shit, I couldn't get you off my mind. I wanted to know if you were okay. I wanted to be there to protect you. I'd do any fuckin' thing you asked me to, Jrue. And I've never allowed someone to have that much power over me, especially after only kissing you."

"The project is done," I blurted out, still breathless from his confession.

"What does that mean?"

"It means that we aren't working together anymore. So, if there were ever a time to act on our feelings for each other, it would be now."

"And what if you can't handle what comes after?"

"I'm a big girl, Kasim. I can take care of myself."

"That should be my job."

"You offering?" I asked, wrapping my arms around his neck.

"Maybe I am."

Kas pressed his tongue against my lips while flattening my spine against the building. His fingertips appraised my curves, hands feeling like satin sliding underneath my too-tight dress. Then he walked his fingertips down the small of my back, stopping to cup my ass as his teeth grazed my neck. I grabbed the sides of his beard, melting into the sweetness of his kiss. My hands danced around his waist and down to the bulge in his pants to squeeze his dick.

"It's so fuckin' big. I want it," I growled.

As big as his dick felt in my hand, I should've been nervous, reluctant even. But the electrifying jolts flowing through my pussy were enough to put those fears aside. He shoved his tongue in my mouth again while massaging my lace-covered clit before shifting my panties to the side. "Mmm. You're already so wet for me."

I moaned as he shoved one of his long, brown fingers inside my warmth. I gently started gyrating my hips back and forth on it.

"Yeah, that's right. Ride that shit," he instructed.

Without warning, he pushed another finger inside me, making me squirm with two times the pleasure. "Shit, your pussy is tight as fuck. I can't wait to put this fuckin' dick inside you," he whispered against my neck as he worked his fingers against my seam. "And when we get to my spot, you can fuck my face as hard as you want to."

My body started shaking. "Ooooh, fuck." I panted.

"Open them pretty ass eyes and tell me this pussy is mine."

My eyes shot open to see him staring me down, anxiously awaiting my climax. "It's y-y-yours."

"Say my name," he whispered before licking and sucking on my earlobe.

"K-Kasim."

OUR MAKE-UP SESSION spilled from the street to inside his car as he navigated us to his place. As ready as I was to experience everything he had to offer, I couldn't wait until we got inside four walls to get the party started. So, I hiked up my dress to slide my panties around my ankles. Kas tore his eyes away from the road long enough to let his thumb strum my clit like a guitar.

"Mmm, shit," I moaned before reaching over to stroke his dick through his pants. Each time I touched it, it felt even bigger than before. "Can I taste it?" I purred, unhooking my seat belt.

Kas gently eased on the brake at a red light before unbuckling his pants and pulling out the main attraction. My teeth flashed white and broad as I watched his dick blossom in front of my eyes.

His dick was everything I thought it would be and more. It was a thick, swollen work of art, standing at attention like a king-sized candy bar. I wasted no time wrapping my lips around the tip and stroking him gently while he tried to keep his focus on the road. His deep, raspy groans echoed through the car as I explored the length of his dick with my tongue. My lips curled around his swollen head as my palms skimmed across his shaft. The muscles in my jaw ticked as Kas fucked the back of my throat. He was so deep I thought I would choke from having his shit damn near tickling my esophagus.

"Goddamn, that shit feels incredible." He howled, gripping the back of my head.

I continued to toy with the tip of his dick until we pulled up to his place. His rough breathing continued as he studied me. "You sure you ready for this? Because after that, I'm about to fuck the shit outta you," he warned.

I placed my hand in his, ready to explore the wild, mind-numbing euphoria that awaited me. "I'm ready," I replied with a smirk before wiping the spit from my lip.

We couldn't keep our hands off each other by the time the elevator opened to his place. Kas made good on his word when we stepped inside by scooping me into his arms and carrying me upstairs. He unhooked my bra with one hand before tossing me on the bed.

"I want you so fuckin' bad right now. Rip my fuckin' clothes off, Kas!"

Minutes later, our clothes lay in piles of haste around the room as we bared our bodies and souls to each other. Eager to feel him inside me, I climbed on top of him. My back stiffened as I eased down on top of him. Pain instantly turned to pleasure as electricity jolted through every nerve ending. My pussy muscles tightened around his girt as I started rolling my hips. His grip around my waist tightened instantly.

"Fuck," he muttered while placing kisses against my collarbone.

His warm hands and lips reached my breasts, kneading over my nipples with his thumbs. He licked circles and figure-eights around my areola before sucking hard and grazing his teeth against my flesh. I smoothed over his strong, protective brown arms as his fingers threaded through my curls, tearing down my updo.

"Oooh shit! Yes! Yes! That feels soooo good." I moaned, hips pumping faster.

He smacked my ass, edging me closer to the delicious moment I'd been waiting for, dreaming about, even. Soon, pleasure poured out of me in waves, liquifying my body as I came. "Ooooh shiiiiiiiittttttt!"

Before I could reclaim my breath, Kas flipped me onto my back and skated his stiffness up and down the seam of my pussy lips like a Slip-N-Slide. Then he buried the head of his thick dick back inside me a few slow strokes at a time. I squirmed with pleasure, ready to explode.

"I want you to worship this dick tonight," Kas stated as his strong hands chained my ankles together over his shoulder before he applied pressure to my G-spot. "Can you do that?"

Kas hovered over me, his gold chain dipping into my mouth as he thrust forward. I gripped his back, digging my nails into his tattooed flesh. "Y-yes," I stammered, unable to control myself.

He expelled his breath in a slow, steady hiss. "Look at me while you take this dick, Jrue."

My pussy pulsated and tingled with pleasure at the sound of his voice. I cracked open my eyes, watching him watch me, unfazed by how unperfect I looked getting fucked underneath him. He looked into my eyes as if he couldn't get enough of me. His hard chest felt like heaven pressed against mine as he thrust deeper into me until my body shook with pleasure. Kas gently pulled out, replacing his dick with his tongue. My spine curved, arching my hips to the ceiling as he placed open-mouth kisses against my warm flesh.

"Ooooh, shitttt!" I screamed, legs squirming wildly underneath him.

Kas gently lashed my clit with his tongue before softly sucking on it. The hair from his beard tickled my inner thighs as I held onto the sides of his face. My screams bounced off the walls. "Yes! Yessss! Oh my fuckin' God, yessss!"

I lost myself inside the sexual eutopia we'd created while he sucked and slurped me as if I was his last meal. He thrust my hips skyward before making a trail of warm, wet saliva from my pussy to my ass. My eyes widened with pleasure when I felt the tip of his tongue flicking my asshole. I'd met my freak match. Not only did he eat the pussy like no one ever had before, but he also munched my groceries with no hesitation. I rocked back and forth, riding his face as his tongue slipped in and out of my asshole.

"Goddamn, my face is so fuckin' wet," he complimented while coming up for air.

Kas propped me up on all fours while caressing and smacking my ass. He dipped back inside me, fucking me like a beast. He gripped my hair, thrusting into me harder and faster as if he'd lost all control. He clutched the back of my neck, and I screamed out in pleasure, gripping the dark sheets.

"Fuck me, Kas! Fuck me like I'm your bitch," I moaned, tearing my lust-filled eyes back at him.

"That's it, take it. Keep takin' it for me."

"I'll take it wherever you want me to!" I promised, silently swearing on my life.

Kas continued to fuck me, each deep stroke splitting me into a million pieces of pleasure. He submerged into me, thrusting in a furious rhythm before a low-pitched growl resounded from his heaving chest. He tensed up, his grip tightening around the indent of my waist. After a few more sweet, deep strokes, he came, shouting as he spilled his seed onto the sheets.

Twenty-Three

CANAAN

MY KNUCKLES COLLIDED against my father's bedroom door. After finding out about his cancer diagnosis and how advanced it was, I'd been waiting for him to meet with me and talk next steps for my succession as head of the McQueen family in *The Order*. He'd been spending most of his time in his room, lying in his bed as if he'd draw his last breath at any moment, but I didn't mind coming to his bedside.

"Come in, Canaan," he instructed, voice sickly.

"You wanted to see me?"

"Yes. I want to talk."

"About what?" I quizzed, inching toward the bed where he lay. He lowered the TV volume to a low murmur before coughing violently. "You aight? Here. Drink some water," I instructed, handing him the glass from his nightstand.

He took a few sips to soothe his throat. "As you can see, I don't have the strength I used to. So, I want you to represent our family at the upcoming *Order* meeting and take over my duties in my absence," he announced.

I dipped my chin to hide the smile on my face. "Anything you need."

"Good. And that's not all."

"Yeah?"

"There's something I need to tell you about me. About this family, b-before I die," he started before another wave of coughing ensued.

"What is it?"

"I have debts to the Rivera family."

"Debts? What kind of debts? Gambling debts?" I asked, leaning in closer. When my questions went too long without being answered, I asked another. "How much do you owe?"

I knew the Rivera family owned a slew of casinos and racetracks throughout New York and Connecticut, and I was also aware of my father's gambling addiction, but I thought that shit was under control.

"Over the years, I've considered Julius Barnes a friend because we've done business together, but I don't trust him," he informed me.

"Why are you telling me this?"

"Because I made a backup deal."

"A backup deal for what? And with who?"

"To settle my debts, a proposal has been brought to the table from Ruiz Rivera for you to marry his youngest daughter, Layla Rivera. She's twenty-one, young, and beautiful. Once you're wed, you will oversee the day-to-day operations in their new casinos."

"You want me to move to New York or Connecticut?" I quizzed.

"No. They will be building new casinos here... on our territory."

My brows heightened. "Our territory? What territory?"

"The same territory I promised to Julius," he confirmed.

"W-what? Why would you do that?"

"My debts are enormous, and my health is failing, Canaan. If something happens to me or your sister doesn't get married before I die, then you will have to marry Layla Rivera."

"And after I marry her, that's it? Your debts to them are forgiven just like that?"

He nodded slowly. "Yes."

"So, you expect me to oversee their casinos *and* represent as the head of this family? Wow, Pop. That's a lot of new responsibility, but I'm ready for it. I've been preparing for this, and I promise you, I won't let you down," I assured him.

"You wouldn't do both."

"Then who—"

"For now, you are my proxy. When I die, Cena will take over as the permanent head of our family and relieve you of your duties."

I scoffed while leaning away from him. "W-what? So I'm a placeholder?"

"You're still playing a key role for this fam—"

"Nah, fuck that!" I yelled, cutting him off. "I've done everything you've ever asked of me, and I'm only good enough to speak for this family while you're still here? Barely fuckin' holding on?"

He mustered up all his strength to sit up in the bed. His dry lips pursed. "You think I owe you something?"

"Yeah, actually, I do."

He cut his tired eyes at me. "You're spoiled, and you're reckless, Canaan. You play the roles I need you to play when I need you to goddamn play them. You should be grateful for the life I've afforded you for the past twenty-five years," he spat before another round of coughing started.

"You know what, fuck you! Fuck *The Order*! Fuck this family! I didn't ask to be born into this shit. I didn't ask for half the shit you put on me, but I took it because I thought we had a fuckin' understanding, Pop!"

"No matter how you may feel, I've made my final wishes known to you, to your sister, and my estate attorney."

I knew that was his way of telling me he'd written his wishes down in his will. There was nothing I could do. It became clear to me that he was only using me to clean up his mess. Shocked that he'd placed the crown on my head only to snatch it right back, I stormed out of his room in a blaze of rage and confusion.

The same territory I'd promised to Julius Barnes, my father had gone around and promised to Ruiz Rivera. It felt like I was both my father and Julius's backup plans, but my father had turned his back on me, making sure that Julius was my *only* plan. It made me wonder if Julius had known of my father's intent all along. It didn't matter regardless. I couldn't let the deal fall through. I'd been selling Trinity the dream that the two of us and Za would be able to be a real family, and then he'd gone and fucked up everything by trying to marry me off to silence his financial demons and giving *my* spot to Cena.

I respected my sister, but I *earned* that spot at the top of the family food chain. Cena was smart, but I'd never considered her for the spot as head of our family, because she'd never gotten her hands dirty before. She never had to. She didn't know what it felt like to have her hands stained in crimson blood. That's what I was for. Besides, it was more my birthright than hers because I was his son.

"Goodnight, Mr. McQueen." His night nurse, Lorraine, greeted me, momentarily snapping me out of my thoughts.

I tipped my head at her before barreling through the front door, too mad to even utter a response. For a second, I thought about leaving everything behind. Why give my all to a family who didn't give a fuck about me? The engine purred as my mind percolated with sinister thoughts. The longer I sat there, the angrier I became. I *knew* tonight would be the night everything I'd been working toward came together seamlessly. If things didn't go my way, I would just have to force them.

I left the driveway before circling the block and parking a few houses down. I stewed in silence for another hour before popping open my center console. I slid on my black gloves and tucked my gun inside the back of my pants before hopping out and jogging down the block. With my father's house in view, I snuck through the back with the spare key and crept toward the kitchen. Lorraine was standing at the island with a small tray of pills in front of her. I wrapped my hand around my back, gripping my gun when I spotted a pair of shears on the far counter. I knew a bullet to the chest would complete the job. Stabbing my father to death would be messy but a lot quieter. Lorraine moved over to the refrigerator to pour a glass of ice-cold water, allowing me to sneak past her and snatch the shears.

I felt the steady pressure of the gun against my back as the door to my father's room creaked open. I slipped inside, ready to make him agree to my terms. My hand slipped over his dry lips, causing his eyes to pop wide.

"Don't say a mothafuckin word," I warned him through my teeth.

I pulled my hand away before gripping the scissors tighter. "All I ever wanted to be was like you. Now, look at me, Pop. Why'd you have to force me to do this? Huh? Why'd you have to force my hand?" I whispered.

His fearful, tired eyes pinged around the room in a panic before landing on mine. "I—I'm ready t-to die," he leaked out.

I wagged my head as a tear slithered down my cheek. "Rest easy, you piece of fuckin' shit."

My arms wavered over my head before I slammed them into his chest, aiming straight for his cold heart. I slowly inched away from his body as the sound of him struggling to draw in his next breath replayed inside my head like a broken record.

"Oh shit. W-what the fuck did I do?"

He wrapped his hands around the shears sticking out of his chest and rolled his eyes to me. The second I reached the door, I made sure I got out of his room by the time they closed. I shuffled down the back, carefully dodging his night nurse. She'd already seen me come in and leave once, and I couldn't risk her seeing me again.

As soon as I landed back inside my car, the first person I called was Julius Barnes. He picked up on the third ring. "Yeah?"

"Boss, it's me. I—I need your help."

Twenty-Four

KAS

2:37 a.m.

I **JOLTED** awake to the violent buzzing sound of my phone vibrating against my nightstand. It wasn't even daylight yet, and Cena was calling. I pressed ignore and snapped my eyes shut before pulling Jrue's warm body into my grasp. Seconds later, the vibrating started again. Nonstop. I rubbed the sleep from my face before answering mid-yawn.

"Yeah?"

"Kas. I need you to meet me at the hospital."

"For what? What's wrong?" I quizzed, my morning voice slow and husky.

"It's my father. He's been stabbed in the—can you just meet me here? Please? It's bad, and I—" Sobs replaced her voice.

"Text me what hospital you're at, and I'm on my way," I said, gaining my feet.

She sniffled. "Okay."

After ending the call, I snapped my neck back at Jrue, who was still sleeping peacefully. I dared not to wake her beautiful ass. Instead, I slipped out of bed and threw on some clothes. While waiting for the elevator to open, I shot Jrue a quick text to let her know I had family business to handle and that I'd have someone deliver breakfast to her and take her home whenever she was ready. I secretly hoped she'd be there whenever I got back, but by the sound of Cena's voice, I knew I'd be tied up by Cena's side with family business for a while.

"KAS!" Cena called out, racing down the hospital corridor to my side.

I met her with a sincere hug before grabbing her shoulders and looking into her puffy, bloodshot eyes. "Cena, what happened? You said on the phone that—"

She looked over her shoulder before cutting me off. "I know what I said."

"Well? What happened? How is your father?"

"He's stable, for now. But the damage is bad, and the doctors don't know if he'll make it through the next few hours. Even if he does, they are afraid that if they take him in for surgery, they'll risk his cancer spreading even more rapidly."

"So what are they going to do?"

"They're monitoring him now, checking him every hour on the hour. And they're flying in a special cardio surgeon from New York. They said he'll be here within the next few hours."

"How are you?"

She shook her head. "I—I don't know. I can't believe they found him with the—"

"What?" I asked, growing more impatient as her silence dragged on.

"Somebody tried to murder my father, Kas. They stabbed him in the chest with fucking kitchen shears! In his sleep! The night nurse found him bleeding out in his bed. The doctors said that if she hadn't called the paramedics when she did, he would've died. He still might. He's holding on by a thread."

My brows raised toward my hairline. "What the fuck? When did all of this happen?"

"Sometime last night."

"Who do you think did it? Does Canaan know? Does *The Order* know?"

"Everyone who needs to know knows, Kas."

"Where's Canaan?"

She twisted her lips before wagging her head. "I don't know. I haven't been able to get in touch with him."

"When's the last time you talked to him?"

Her head drooped as she answered. "Yesterday before all of this happened."

"Have you spoken to your father to see if he remembers anything?"

Her head wagged from left to right. "No. I haven't been able to speak to him. Only hold his hand."

"What about the night nurse? Did you talk to her? Did she see anything or anyone?"

"She said it was early when he told her he was going upstairs to his room, but lately, that's nothing new. He's been so tired these days that he's almost always in there. After noticing he left his pills on the kitchen counter, she said she poured him a glass of ice water and took his pills up to him. When she got upstairs, she noticed the door was partially cracked open but didn't think anything of it. Then when she walked in his room, she saw him bleeding out, stabbed in the chest with a pair of fuckin' shears."

I lowered my head. "Damn. Is there anything I can do?"

"You got a time machine?" she quizzed, wiping her tears.

"I wish I did."

"I just didn't think it would come to this. The cancer was bad enough. Now attempted murder?"

I continued to dig for information. "Have the cops been here yet?"

"Two detectives came by and spoke with me after speaking with his night nurse. I didn't have anything to give them. I keep kicking myself because I knew I should've stayed there that night, and I didn't. I went home."

"You can't wear the blame on your shoulders for this. You're right where you need to be."

She loosely shrugged her shoulders. "Yeah, I guess."

"Where did you say Canaan was again?"

"I didn't. I haven't heard from him or my father since yesterday."

"And you don't know if the two of them saw each other?"

Our eyes met at the same time. "What are you trying to say?"

"I'm not saying anything," I stated. "I'm only asking questions."

"We both know my brother is a loose cannon, but he doesn't have anything to do with this. He c-couldn't," she trembled.

I bobbed my head in long, contemplative lines. "Okay."

"You think otherwise?"

"If I'm bein' honest, I don't know what the fuck to think right now."

"Yeah, well, I guess that makes two of us. But uh, listen. I'm about to go back in there and sit with him until the surgeon gets here."

"You want me to come with you?" I offered.

She shook her head. "No. Thanks for coming when I called."

"You're welcome. You sure you don't want me to stay?"

She shook her head again. "No. Go inform your family and let me know if you hear from my brother."

"Okay. Keep me posted on your father and let me know if you need anything. I mean that."

She looked down at her phone. "Oh. Hold on. This is him calling me now. Hello? Canaan?" She answered before darting down the hallway.

I LEFT the hospital and headed to see my father and give him the news in person. The minute I pulled up next to Kamil's car, I witnessed Canaan speeding out of the driveway. Curious about why he was there, I went inside to ask my father and Kamil what the hell was going on.

"Kas, I'm glad you're here." My father greeted me when I barged through his study doors.

"What the hell is goin' on? Why was Canaan McQueen speeding out of the driveway like a bat out of fuckin' hell?"

"Sit down. There's something I need to tell you. It's about his father."

"Oh, I know. I was just with Cena at the hospital. She told me somebody tried to murder him—stabbed him in the chest with scissors."

"He's dead, Kasim."

"W-what? Fuckouttahere. Nah. I *just* left the hospital and came straight here."

"Canaan was here on the phone with Cena when it happened. He succumbed to his injuries," Kamil added.

"Now everyone is in question, especially our family," my father stated.

My forehead creased in confusion. "Why? Because of the deal you made with the Simms family? I thought you said no one knew about that."

"No one does, and they can't find out. If anyone did, they'd think I had something to do with this. If word spreads through the organization, we'll lose all control."

"But we didn't," Kamil paused, "right?"

We eyed our father closely, awaiting his answer, both of us silently praying the answer was no. "No. Of course not. In some ways, I consider Silas one of my oldest friends."

Kamil sighed. "Okay then, Pa. Then what's the problem?"

"Because of our relationship, we need to seal our end of the deal to ensure our family retains the respect of every family under *The Order* umbrella. Plus, they'll need our family's protection more than ever now."

"Why should any of that matter anymore? He's dead. What's the rush now?" I butted in.

Before he could answer, the phone rang. "I have to take this," he stated.

Kamil and I stood in the foyer in silence while our father stepped away to have a private conversation. He returned several minutes later with a stern look on his face. "Who was that?" Kamil asked.

"They are making Silas's funeral arrangements for early next week."

"Okay."

"And since all the families will be coming into the city to attend, we think it's best to move the wedding up again."

My brows jutted toward my hairline. "What?"

"To next weekend," he concluded.

My heart plummeted to my feet the minute I heard the news. "Nah. No! Hell no!"

"I told you I *need* that territory. It's not going to be a sealed deal until you hold up your end of the deal for this family!"

"What makes you so sure me marrying Cena will get you what you want, huh?"

"Arrangements have been made," he answered allusively.

Glaring anger poured from my eyes. "With who? Huh? This is my life! Tell me the truth!"

"With Canaan McQueen."

"Is that why he was here before I got here?" Kamil asked.

"What the fuck aren't you tellin' us, Pa?"

"Silas and I had been discussing my intent to expand long before he came to me with the news about his health. After that, all conversations on my expansion stalled. Even still, he came to me for loans to help pay off his gambling debts to Ruiz Rivera. Kas, you and I had the conversation already. When he asked for the money, I refused him initially. But I knew he wanted more than that. He was weak—all his business dealings were like a ticking time bomb. He was liquidating his assets. So, in exchange for the money, he proposed a marriage between Koda and Cena for strength. So again, I brought up the territory, and we agreed that when the wedding happened, more than what I originally asked for would be mine."

"Where does Canaan fit into all of this?" I questioned.

"Once the Simms family moved in on the territory too early, I knew that if I didn't offer up a replacement for Koda, he wouldn't get the loan, and I wouldn't get the territory. So, I reached out to Canaan. There was no surprise in his interest and intent on taking over for his father whenever his body surrendered to his sickness."

My brow raised. "Did you know that Silas wants Cena to take over as the head of the McQueen family? Not Canaan, Pa!"

"She told you that?" Kamil asked.

I scoffed. "Who else?"

My father's eyes widened, informing me that he didn't know that piece of information. "W-what?"

"Did you know that Silas wanted Cena to head their family?" Kamil asked.

"No, but I agreed that if it came down to a fight between them, I'd help him get the votes he'd need to secure his spot as the head of his family."

"And in return, you get the territory you need to expand our dealings," Kamil answered.

"And maybe without having to give Silas the money for the loan," I grumbled, putting the pieces together.

Pa nodded. "Yes."

"And what about Douglass Simms? Has he handled his number two? Did he get him in line?"

"Don't worry about him. I have him right where I want him for now."

I gritted my teeth for control as the heat of anger burned my face. All he'd done was show me that we were nothing more than pawns he was moving across the board whenever and wherever he felt like it. One thing was for sure: My worst enemies couldn't compete with the snakes in my fuckin' bloodline. Silas and my father were cut from the same cloth because of their thirst for power and control, but my father didn't know a damn thing about Cena McQueen. I'd made the mistake of underestimating her once. I wouldn't do it again.

Unable to control my rage, I confronted him. "All this shit could've been avoided if you had just talked to me! We could've come up with a plan everybody fuckin' benefitted from, but you're selfish, and you're only thinkin' about your fuckin' self and what you want!" I roared.

Pa shot a glare up to silence me, and Kamil jumped in to calm me down. "Kas."

"Nah. Fuck that. You don't give a fuck about this family or me! You were just trying to cover your own ass!"

"Get him out of here! Get him out of here before I kill him myself!" my father yelled.

"You need me too much! You ain't gon' do shit to me!" I spat.

Kamil tried to grab me, but I shoved him off before pushing through his study doors. My pace didn't stop until I was back inside my car. The engine rumbled as I whipped out my phone to see a text from Cena.

Cena: *He's gone. He just died.*

Me: *I'm so sorry. I know this is a bad time, but can we meet? There's something you need to know.*

Cena: *Yeah.*

I tossed the phone in my passenger seat and sped down the driveway. I knew Cena would be knee-deep in grief over the loss of her father, but she needed to know about her brother's intent to fight her for their father's seat.

I'd been so wrapped up in family business that I hadn't responded to Jrue's text. I'd already fallen too deep for her. Now that we'd taken things to the next level, I knew the time had come to tell her the truth about my family, Cena, and our inescapable marriage. As crazy as it sounded, I prayed that when she found out the truth about me and my dark side, she'd decide to stick around. I didn't care what I had to do or *not do* to keep her around. I wasn't willing to let her go.

Twenty-Five

JRUE

8:27 a.m.

MY EYELIDS FLUTTERED open as a wide yawn stretched my mouth into an O shape. I lazily flopped back against the sea of black pillows, my lower body still heavy and relaxed. After finding my phone, I saw Kas's name across the screen.

Kas: *Good morning, beautiful. I had some family business to handle. Take a look at this menu and order whatever you want for breakfast. I'll have someone deliver it to you and have a driver take you home whenever you're ready.*

A wide smile stretched across my face before I texted him back.

Me: *Hurry back. I woke up wet for you this morning.*

I pressed send before locking the phone and rolling over to grab his pillow to cuddle my chest. I planned to text him something spicy and then leave him on read, hoping he'd cut his business short and toss me around another time or two. The text wasn't a lie. Just thinking about Kasim got me wet. He didn't have to touch me, tease me, or even taste me to turn me on. All he had to do was be himself. *He* was the main attraction. My skin prickled as I closed my eyes and let flashbacks of the night flood my brain. His sex was like a '90s slow jam. And that dick?

142

He had the type of wood that required a few stretches before taking it on. It was the most beautiful piece of hard, brown flesh I'd ever seen. And the way he licked my pussy and my ass like they were his last meal? *Mmm.* I didn't need to see my reflection to know I had the afterglow of sex on my face. I was ready and willing to tattoo his name all over my body.

After deciding to take my time and wait for him to come back, I unlocked my phone again to check out the menu link he'd sent and my email. My eyes popped wide when I saw over fifteen unread emails with service inquiries.

"Holy fuckin' shit," I muttered.

Everyone who'd inquired had all been at the mixer and admired my work. Excited as hell, I called Kas to share the news. The phone rang twice before he sent me to voicemail, but I quickly brushed it off.

AFTER EATING AND SHOWERING, I left Kas's place three and a half hours later and returned home to dish with Yara about my night. The minute the door snapped closed behind me, I caught Yara's eyes on me from the kitchen.

"You fucked around and found out with WorkBae, didn't you?" she probed, arms folded across her chest.

As badly as I wanted to, I couldn't control the smile slowly spreading across my face. "I did."

"And?"

"What?" I quizzed with an airy shrug.

"Was it worth it?"

"Oh, it was *definitely* worth it," I assured her with a nod.

"Well, now I have to hear more. I need to know about the girth, length, tongue game, and positions. Tell me *everything*." Yara gushed.

I giggled before crashing across the couch and letting my body sink into the cushions. "Whhhhyyyyy are you this nosy?"

"Because I'm getting ready to agree to sit on one dick for the rest of my life, remember? So I've gotta live vicariously through you!"

"I mean, what can I say? It was the best dick I've ever had in my life."

"Mmm. What made it good? The stroke? The length? The width?"

"Everything. The tongue. The dick. The stroke game. Everything was like a fuckin' well-oiled machine, like, oh my God. I'm hooked. Like, I think I know what it feels like to be on crack," I confessed, followed by a huff of laughter.

"Okay, so I'm hearing all good things."

"Not good, my dear friend, unprecedented. Shit, unrivaled."

"*Sensational*," she said in her best imitation of Future.

"Seriously, Ya-Ya. Like, the dick was so good it needs to be celebrated. It should have its own national day."

"Three cheers to WorkBae's illustrious, noteworthy, highly revered big, black dick!" Yara cackled.

"Here, here!"

"I'm happy you got yourself some good wood. You deserve it, friend."

"Man, it was so worth the wait. Like, his dick is my new happy place. He ate my pussy so damn good and then turned me over and ate my ass, girl. I thought I was gonna dieeeee."

Yara's brows shot to her baby hairs. "Damn, he ate the kitty and the groceries on the first night. I'm impressed and loving everything about this man so far. Wait, do I even know his name? I've been calling him WorkBae for so long; I can't remember if you even told me," she said with a giggle.

"Yeah, I don't know that I feel right changing his name from WorkBae in your head. But his name's—"

"Oh, wait! Wait! Hold that thought!" Yara yelled while holding up her index finger to pause our conversation. "It's Blake. I gotta take it. Sorry, one second."

She skated down the hallway with her cell glued to her ear, and I rechecked my phone—still nothing from Kas. I pushed out a loud sigh and flopped my head against the nearest throw pillow when I heard Yara's footsteps trampling over to me.

"I'm so pissed right now!"

I sat up on my elbows. "Why? What happened?"

"I have to freaking leave! You remember the bride with the big-ass budget and the ghost fiancé I told you about?"

"Yeah. What about them?"

"Well, they just called an emergency lunch meeting with Blake and me to discuss moving up the damn wedding *again,* so I've gotta go. The meeting is in like forty-five minutes."

"It's okay. We'll finish talking when you get back," I promised.

"Tell you what. Let's meet for a late lunch in about another hour or so. And you can finish spillin' all the WorkBae tea, then? Besides, there's something I need to tell you."

"What is it?"

"I can't get into it now. We'll finish later!"

"Okay, cool. Where?"

"I'll text you the place where we're meeting, and you can just meet me there. Just grab a table on the opposite side of the restaurant, so I don't look unprofessional," she said with a wink.

"Sounds good."

"Ugh. Let me go get dressed." Yara groaned.

"Maybe it won't be all bad."

She shrugged. "At least it sounds like we're finally going to get to meet her mystery fiancé. Truthfully, I was beginning to think the man didn't exist."

I chuckled. "See! Silver lining. I'll see you in a little bit."

TWO HOURS LATER, I was going to meet Yara at the restaurant to finish telling her all about Kas and me. His scent had been washed from my curves, but the relaxed feeling remained, and I hadn't been able to erase the smile I'd been wearing since I woke up. As thoughts of him began to overflow my mind, I whipped out my phone to text him.

Me: *You good?*

After throwing on some clothes and fixing my hair, I trekked to the car. The engine hummed while I quickly texted Yara to tell her I was on the way.

Me: *Heading your way now.*

Yara: *Cool. Wrapping up soon. It should be done by the time you get here.*

Halfway to the restaurant, my phone buzzed with a response from Kas, and I let out a breath I didn't know I'd been holding.

Kas: *I'm sorry I got caught up. Are you still at my spot? We need to talk.*

Me: *No. Meeting a friend for lunch. Can we meet up later?*

Kas: *Yeah.*

I slid my phone inside my bag before getting out and walking a few blocks to the restaurant. Once inside, I spotted Yara at the back of the restaurant, waving me down with a smile chiseled into her features. As I approached her, I saw Yara and her boss shaking hands with a couple before they turned around. My blood ran cold, freezing me in place when I saw their faces.

"Hey, Jrue, over here," Yara called out.

My legs felt like sandbags as I slowly inched toward them. "Hey. Jrue, these are our clients, Cena McQueen, and her fiancé, Kasim Barnes. These two are tying the knot *next* weekend," she announced.

My breath hitched as my eyes dropped to the large rock on top of her finger before shooting up to Kas. "W-what?"

TO BE CONTINUED...

Afterword

A note from K.L. Hall.
Reader,

Thank you for reading *Crushed Velvet & Cashmere*. If you've made it this far, I hope you'll consider taking a minute to tell me what you thought about the book in the form of a **review and/or rating**. Don't hesitate to let me know what you'd like to see from me next! I thoroughly enjoy reading your thoughts and hearing from you as well! I'm always striving to attract new and retain current readers, and reviews are one of the easiest ways to attract readers. Tell a friend if you loved the book, and most importantly, let me know!

All my love,
K.L. Hall

About the Author

K.L. Hall is a national bestselling and award-winning author. As a serial storyteller, Hall has penned over three dozen titles in various genres—including African American urban fiction and romance, paranormal, children's books (as Kimberley M.), and non-fiction. Her fictional stories straddle the intersection of classic Urban and spell-binding Romance.

Highly Acclaimed Titles:

In the Arms of a Savage: (Peaked at #1 in Women's Fiction)

The Potomac Falls Series (Peaked at #1 and #2 in African American Erotica)

Sign up for my mailing list to stay updated with new releases, giveaways, sneak peeks, and more! Click this link: https://bit.ly/38RMpV5 *(E-Book Only)*

Connect with me on social media:

Facebook: https://www.facebook.com/authorklhall

Twitter: https://twitter.com/authorklhall

Instagram: https://www.instagram.com/officialklhall/

Website: https://www.authorklhall.com

Other novels by K.L. Hall:

Diary of a Hood Princess 1-3

Rise of a Street King: The Justice Silva Story *(Spin-Off to the Diary of a Hood Princess series)*

Broken Condoms and Promises 1-3

In the Arms of a Savage 1-3

Built for a Savage: Blaze and Camille's Love Story *(Spin-Off to the In the Arms of a Savage Series)*

A Ruthle$$ Love Story 1-3

Fallin' for the Alpha of the Streets 1-2

The Most Savage of Them All: The Wolfe Calloway Story *(Prequel to the In the Arms of a Savage Series)*

When a Gangsta Loves a Good Girl

Caught Between my Husband and a Hustler

The Illest Taboo 1-2

To the Only Thug I'll Ever Love

A Lover's Heist: Chief and Gianna's Love Story

A Lover's Heist II: Rome and Lira's Love Story

A Lover's Heist III: Baby and Skai's Love Story

Crushed Velvet and Cashmere

Short Reads + Novellas:

Bi-Curious: An Erotic Tale

Bi-Curious 2: Tastes Like Candy

House of Cards 1-2

A Savage Calloway Christmas *(Christmas novella to the In the Arms of a Savage Series)*

Lovin' the Alpha of the Streets: A Valentine's Day Novella *(Valentine's Day novella to the Fallin' for the Alpha of the Streets Series)*

Awakened: A Paranormal Romance

As Long as You Stay Down

Solace in Seven

Solace II: The Final Cut

Something Bleu

Something Borrowed

Something New

The Knight Before Christmas: A Potomac Falls Short

I'll Be Home for Christmas: A Potomac Falls Short Book II

Children's Books:

Princess for Hire

Princess Twinkle Toes & the Missing Magic Sneakers

Little One, Change the World

Adjust Your Crown: A Self-Love Coloring Book for Children of Color

Non-Fiction:

Authors are a Business: The Booked & Busy Course Mini Book

www.ingramcontent.com/pod-product-compliance
Lightning Source LLC
Chambersburg PA
CBHW071435130726
47997CB00006B/2102